A LIGHT IN THE DESERT

A Novel

A LIGHT IN THE DESERT

A Novel

ANNE MONTGOMERY

Blank Slate Press | St. Louis, MO

Blank Slate Press | Saint Louis, MO 63116

For information, contact:
Blank Slate Press
An imprint of Amphorae Publishing Group
a woman- and veteran-owned business
4168 Hartford Street, Saint Louis, MO 63116

Manufactured in the United States of America
Set in Milo and Adobe Garamond Pro
Interior designed by Kristina Blank Makansi
Cover Design by Kristina Blank Makansi

Library of Congress Control Number: 2018946954
ISBN: 9781732139114

This book was inspired by and is dedicated to my dear friend Sergeant Don Clarkson, a Green Beret who served in Vietnam with the 9th Infantry ARVN Soldiers from December 1968 to November 1970. Don died in 2010 from complications of Post-Traumatic Stress Disorder and Agent Orange poisoning.

For you are all children of light, children of the day.
We are not of the night or of the darkness.
—1 Thessalonians 5:5

Do not remember the sins of my youth, nor my
transgressions;
According to Your mercy remember me ...
Look on my affliction and my pain,
And forgive all my sins.
—Psalm 25

BEFORE

ARIZONA, 1995

THE MOONLIGHT ILLUMINATED the desert floor as the boys walked along the tracks. A single voice, loud and brash, carried easily down the sandy wash and up the side of the ragged mound of basalt where the man lay hidden. Belly down on the jumble of volcanic rocks, he watched and listened, just like he'd been trained.

"Fuck 'em!" the larger boy cried, slinging a beer can at a nearby saguaro. The alcohol and weed, as usual, made him agitated. Anger would come next.

With his binoculars, the man saw an amateurish tattoo resembling some sort of cat on the boy's upper left arm. A faded flannel shirt—unbuttoned, sleeves ripped out—fluttered open as he marched across the trestle, baring his pale chest to the warm desert air. The other boy, much smaller and darker, walked a good ten yards behind, hands deep in his pockets, head down as if slowly counting the railroad ties as he went.

Rocks pressed into the man's body, but he had learned long ago to will away physical pain. He remained perfectly still, blending into the mountain that, even when the harsh desert sun shone at its brightest, was known for its blackness.

"He'll get his!" the larger boy barked. He reached down, gripping a thick, rusted eight-inch nail—an iron railroad spike—and hurled it into the wash thirty feet below.

Only when the boys had been enveloped by the darkness far down the track did the man finally stand and slip silently into the night.

1

KELLY GARCIA SAT CROSS-LEGGED before the dusty grave, a cluster of blood-red bougainvillea in her lap. She finished the last orange wedge and, remembering the compost heap, stuffed the peel inside the front pocket of her faded sundress, the fabric of which strained to cover her bulging belly.

It wasn't the first time Kelly had visited the graves of the tiny ones. The metal crosses, which had finally replaced the crumbling wooden ones, marked the graves of Maria and Gregorita Amabisca, infants born in the Gila River Valley not long after the turn of the century, neither of whom had survived even one month in the living world. Where were the infants' little spirits now? Had they gone? Or did they spend their days here, hiding behind the old gravestones and scattered creosote bushes? Were they tiny, elf-like creatures, darting about like butterflies but always just out of sight? Or had they, as the Children explained, been lifted off to Paradise?

She felt the baby move. Would her child live long enough to grow up or would God take the baby to heaven instead? If the child was born with a face like hers, perhaps floating in the clouds with the angels would be better. Angels, she knew, must certainly be kinder than people.

She reached over and touched the polished pink granite stone covering her father's grave. Money was scarce, but when the uniformed men arrived, they said her father had been a war hero. They handed her mother a folded American flag and made sure Bryan Kelly received a proper burial and a grave marker. Now his tarnished Silver Star, attached to its red, white and blue ribbon, rested in a velvet box under Kelly's bed.

She traced the letters spelling out her father's surname. Her last name was no longer Kelly. His quirky sense of humor had rendered her Kelly Kelly, but after he stuck the gun in his mouth, her mother had insisted that Kelly Kelly was not a suitable name, blaming the appellation on her father's Irishness, and demanding she take the name of her stepfather.

A hot breeze from the flat, sparsely cultivated land south of the cemetery lifted dust and grit, blowing Kelly's ink-black hair away from her damaged face. Her father always smiled when saying her name. Kelly Kelly made a happy sound, he said, like bird song or a cricket's chirp. All she had left of him now were the medal, the grave, and the odd blue eyes that struggled against her dark features. The long straight hair was a gift from her mother's Maricopa ancestors. Her face? No one was sure where that had come from.

Kelly looked up. The sun was sinking down behind the mountains, shooting streaks of light across the Sonoran Desert sky and dying the clouds the color of pink and purple Easter eggs.

Suddenly, she realized she was late for dinner. The Children of the Light did everything on schedule, so she had to hurry. She picked up the bougainvillea branches that would grace the communal dining table and pushed herself off the ground. Momentarily losing her balance, she clutched the branches tightly and felt a thorn prick her finger. She wished the baby would come soon. She was tired of feeling awkward. So as not to stain her dress, she quickly sucked the blood that oozed from the wound, then turned and walked up the dirt road that wound back to the compound.

2

JASON RAMM DROPPED the box of battered bricks into the bed of his truck. He turned to make another trip up the hill to one of the Rowley Mine's tumbled-down out buildings when he heard soft moaning. Ramm stepped over rocky ground as quietly as he could and stopped at the edge of the mine's main shaft. Cool air rushed from the gaping hole. He crouched, tipping the brown, dirt-encrusted cowboy hat back on his head as he stared into the darkness.

The whimpering continued.

The inch-thick, iron cable—left from the mine's working days—was rusty and twisted, but Ramm knew it was still secure. He grabbed hold and edged his way down the shaft. The wall of the Rowley Mine had a sixty-percent incline, but was fairly simple for him to negotiate, especially when compared to some of the jagged cliffs and man-made structures he had rappelled in the past. A two-foot band of turquoise-colored chrysocolla guided him as he dropped about forty feet to where the shaft floor leveled. He stood, but at six-foot-three, he had to stoop to keep from hitting his head on the rock ceiling.

He saw the dog crumpled in the corner. Was it some feral thing, perhaps the offspring of a coyote and a wild dog, the kind of animal many ranchers in the area shot on sight? Ramm edged closer, fully aware of the damage a wounded creature could inflict. He spotted the barbed wire wrapped tightly around the dog's legs and torso and instinctively drew the six-inch blade he wore strapped to his belt. A quick slice would end the animal's suffering.

Later, Ramm struggled on the uneven shaft and shifted the weight of the old parka slung over his back. The dog whimpered and Ramm whispered, "Hold on. It'll be okay."

Finally, he pulled himself up over the lip of the mine and laid the dog on the pebbled ground in the bright Arizona sunlight. He estimated the animal weighed about seventy pounds, not much less than that Texas boy he'd carried out of the jungle who, thanks to a mortar round, had lost much of his bulk when both legs had been blown off at the hip. Ramm examined the tightly-wound barbed wire. He thought again about slitting the creature's throat, but the animal had a strong heartbeat, and he was weary of killing. He hoisted the dog into his arms and walked toward the truck.

Back at his place, Ramm carefully cut the barbed wire which overlapped crazily and cut deeply into the dog's flesh. Eventually, he managed to snip the metal into small pieces that he extracted. When the dog's legs slipped free of the binding, Ramm saw that she was female and that she had been tortured. Crude swastika carvings bloodied her belly. Some of Ramm's peers in Vietnam had often marked their prey, identifying the deceased as a product of their work, but that had never been his style.

He was glad the dog was unconscious as he cleaned and disinfected the wounds. The wire cuts and carvings on her belly were not life threatening, but she also had a large swollen spot, probably incurred in the fall down the shaft, on the left side of her head. And her right front leg was broken. The fracture appeared to be several weeks old. Was that the reason her tormentors had been able to catch her?

While he bathed the dog, he noticed faint markings on her neck for the first time. She had once worn a collar. Had she been dumped in the desert like so many others? Animals left to forage for themselves or link up with a pack, if they were lucky. For most, abandonment meant a cruel death by starvation, dehydration, or poison. The fortunate ones never survived the interstate.

The dog slept for several hours and Ramm was careful to not make any sudden movements or loud noises. After she woke, he sat on the front steps of his cabin with a plate of cooked chicken.

"Good girl," he said when the dog finally accepted food from his hand. He put another piece of chicken in his palm and held it out. With the exception of a slightly bent front leg, she'd recover from the abuse.

Together, they finished the chicken and Ramm put the plate on the bottom step for the dog to lick. When she was done, she curled up next to him, looking up at him with deep brown eyes.

"Who did this to you?" he said, scratching the dog's neck. He didn't put his own killing in the same category as those who harmed animals. He didn't torture his victims. When he killed, the moment of impact, regardless of the weapon, was instantaneous, and he believed quite painless. He prided himself on neat, clean finishes.

The dog, favoring the bad leg, hobbled into the yard. She sniffed around the base of a spidery ocotillo, then relieved herself near a black basalt boulder. Ramm leaned back and watched as the Sonoran Desert sky provided another evening light show over the distant mountains. He'd come here looking for peace. He'd had so little in his life. The dog nudged his hand.

"Tomorrow, I'll get you some real food, Dog. No more cooked chicken for you. Don't want you getting spoiled."

3

THE SCREEN DOOR of Hyder's Butterfield General Store banged shut behind Ramm, jingling the brass cowbell. Behind the counter, Tom Pace raised his hand in a friendly greeting. "Hey, stranger. Haven't seen you in a couple a weeks."

"Been workin' on the house. Collecting those old bricks from what's left of the Rowley Mine structure. I hope to finish up the fireplace in the next couple of days." Ramm took the cardboard box the shop owner handed him and began filling it with groceries.

"Better watch the company that owns the place don't catch you shaggin' them bricks. You'll get fined for sure."

Ramm smiled as he reached for a five-pound sack of sugar. "I'm not worried." He dismissed Tom's comment because he was the company. The Rowley Mine and the surrounding two hundred acres of desert wilderness belonged to him, but if anyone tried to find out who the owner was, they'd get tangled in a labyrinthine web of corporations. He'd made sure of that. No one would find his name on anything.

Ramm loaded the cardboard box with bacon, eggs, five pounds of flour, coffee, frozen chicken parts, hamburger, cereal, milk, and a pound of butter. Since his appetite seemed to be coming back, he wished he could get a nice fillet, maybe some seafood. Fresh tuna steak, thinly sliced, slightly seared, with some soy sauce and wasabi. He was hungry. But Ramm knew better than to ask for any of those items at the Butterfield General Store. Not only would Tom Pace not stock such things, Ramm wanted to make sure no one thought he was anything other than what he appeared to be.

After placing his groceries on the counter, he picked up another empty box.

"Let me guess," the storeowner said. "I'll bet there'll be no meat in that box." Tom grinned, exposing a missing upper tooth. "They wanna be vegetarians, that's their business, ya know? But that not-havin'-sex-thing. I'm not sure I could do that."

Ramm burst out laughing, probably the first time he'd done so spontaneously in years. Maybe the desert was doing him some good. "Shit, Tom! When's the last time you had sex with someone other than your own right hand?"

Tom laughed. "Well, ya know, Hyder ain't got many eligible ladies."

"Just a bunch of old drunks and a few of us diehard cowboys. And the Children."

"Guess it keeps us outta trouble," the shopkeeper grinned.

"Oh! I almost forgot. You got any of those big sacks of dog food?"

"Got yourself a dog?"

"No, Tom. I'm gonna feed it to Becky. And speaking of my horse, I'm getting low on feed. Can you order me some?"

"Okay, don't tell me."

Ramm watched Tom scribble on the yellow pad by the register. The grizzled storeowner was the town gossip. The man knew everything about everybody, and Ramm had utilized this predilection extensively when he'd first come to Hyder to hide. He'd fed the man information setting up a cover he knew Tom would spread around to anyone in the area who would listen. All the talk had made Ramm's acceptance in the tiny desert town that much easier.

When the groceries were tightly packed in several cardboard boxes, the two men carried them outside.

"She's out in the truck," Ramm said, nodding toward the unobtrusive brown pickup. "I found her in the Rowley Mine's main shaft. Someone cut her up, wrapped her in barbed wire, and dumped her. I call her Dog."

"That's original." Tom shook his head. He had no wife or children, but he did have two mongrel dogs that were as devoted to him as he was to them. "What kinda assholes would do a thing like that? Can't imagine."

Ramm shook his head. "Me either."

After stowing the supplies in the bed of the truck, Ramm climbed in, waved goodbye, and pulled onto the one-lane road that fronted the store and ran parallel with the Southern Pacific Railroad tracks.

Moments later, he passed an old man towing an ancient nag with a rope halter. Tom had told him Nunzio had been a miner and a migrant farmhand. Now he wandered the area, dragging that old roan around packed to the hilt with all his belongings. Hyder's version of a vagrant.

Ramm had traveled several miles when he noticed the smoke. He steered the truck onto the south shoulder of the road and watched as thick black coils rose like twisting cobras, blotting out the clear, blue desert sky. Fire leaped from the wooden railroad overpass, one of hundreds between Phoenix and Los Angeles. A creosote bush burst into flames, oily leaves igniting *en masse.*

Ramm stared into the fire. What had started the blaze in such a desolate place? Lightning was out. The country road, a straight black ribbon with views of nothing but dusty desert scrub, rarely drew visitors, and locals certainly knew better than to toss a lighted cigarette to the ground. Besides, on a windless day like this, a burning butt could not travel the twenty-five yards out to the trestle.

Sooty smoke enveloped the tracks as brilliant orange flames danced on desiccated desert foliage. Adrenaline surged through Ramm. Did he see something moving? Frantically, he scanned the scene again. Now he saw the blond boy clearly, face blackened, limping out of the swirling smoke, bloody stumps where his hands had been. The familiar stench of burning flesh hit Ramm with the force of a live grenade.

"Kill me!" the boy pleaded in a strangely toneless voice. "For God's sake! Kill me!"

Ramm's hands gripped the wheel. He squeezed his eyes shut. Sweat soaked his T-shirt. He forced himself to breathe deeply, tried to will the panic away. Finally, he opened his eyes.

4

"EXCUSE ME, but I think you should see this."

Buck James, the owner of the only gas station in Dateland, glanced over the top of his sports page at the plump, fortyish, shirt and tie in the doorway. "That'll be fifteen even for the gas."

"Okay. Right. But I really think you need to take a look in your restroom."

Buck eased his bulk off the ripped black Naugahyde barstool, knowing the city boy was probably freaking over something stupid. A spider, maybe, or a little snake.

"It's right over there. In the bathroom. By the sink." The man stepped back and pointed.

Buck walked over and grabbed the latch. Paint, faded by the desert sun and of no discernible color, etched the door with spidery cracks. Buck glanced at the man, smiled, and opened the door.

"It's dynamite, isn't it?"

"I'll take care of it," the station owner answered, flinging his cigarette to the ground by the door. He crushed the butt with the heel of his battered work boot. "You move on now."

"But—"

"But what, buddy? Didn't you hear me? Just give me the fifteen bucks for the gas and get the hell out of here. I'll take care of it. Move!"

ψ

"You little fuck!" Buck ripped open the trailer door and grabbed Billy before he had a chance to run.

"You gonna blow up your own daddy, boy? Don't have the balls to take me on face-to-face?"

Buck hurled Billy onto a faded blue Formica table. A cup of cold coffee and a half-eaten bowl of cereal—warm milk being nursed by flies—splashed to the grimy vinyl floor. Fist clenched, Buck reared back. It was a tableau Billy had seen countless times, and he was ready for it. He ducked his head, slipping from Buck's grasp just as his father's hand slammed into the trailer wall.

"Shit! You little prick!" The much-scarred skin on Buck's knuckles was ripped back. Blood streamed down his fingers onto the floor.

Billy, on all fours, scooted out of reach. He saw sky through the open doorway and bolted for the ancient blue Chevy waiting in the dusty drive, knowing Buck could never catch him in a footrace. Luckily, he was prepared. The key was in the ignition, and the car was packed with food, hunting gear, and anything he could find that might be the least bit useful. He'd cleaned Buck out.

Billy wrenched open the car door and glanced over his shoulder. Buck stood breathing heavily in the trailer's doorway, blood dripping from his wounded hand.

"Don't you fuckin' come back here! Go runnin' to your momma, the cheatin' spic whore." Buck started toward him.

Billy turned the key and the engine coughed. He tried again, and this time she turned over. He floored the accelerator. If only that stupid guy hadn't gone in to use the can, Billy would have finished what he started, and wasted his sorry excuse-of-a-dad by now.

The car roared down the road picking up speed. Billy glanced into the rearview mirror and could see Buck in the driveway holding his mangled hand, hurling expletives at his only child.

It didn't matter now. Billy had what he'd come back for. The two brown cartons were safely stowed in the trunk.

ψ

"Buck!"

Jack Cooper slammed the door on his white Yuma County Sheriff's Department Blazer. The AC was acting up again. Non-desert dwellers swore that white cars were cooler in the blazing heat. But hot was hot, no matter what color vehicle you drove.

A door swung open. "Hey, Coop. What's up?" Buck exited the bathroom, drying his hands with a paper towel.

Cooper noticed the mangled knuckles, but said nothing. Then, he followed Buck into the station and watched him settle on his customary stool behind the counter. "Got something you'd like to tell me?"

Buck glanced down at a girly magazine that was open to a centerfold spread.

Cooper crossed his arms. "Well?"

"Wasn't nothin', Coop, but I guess that city boy just couldn't keep his mouth shut."

"You're tellin' me a couple sticks of dynamite tucked under the sink in your bathroom 'wasn't nothin'?"

"Probably just dropped there by accident."

"Yeah, right. Where is it?"

"Out back."

"I'm guessing you have no reason to need dynamite, and no permit allowing you to possess it," Cooper said.

"Nope. But it's not mine. And I was gonna take care of it."

"Whadya say we take care of it now?"

Five minutes later, the deputy lit the fuse and hustled back to the hulking station owner who stood with his hands in his pockets. Buck's ratty cowboy hat was squashed on his head, shielding dark eyes nature had placed just a little too close together. It was not an impressive explosion, as far as they go. And if anyone asked, Cooper would have had to admit there was really no need to blow up the dynamite. He just didn't want to have to transport it.

"Who do you think 'dropped' it in your bathroom, Buck?" Cooper asked when the all-too-brief fireworks display ended.

"I already told you. I don't know."

"Try again."

Buck coughed and spit a green glob into the dirt. "Coulda been my boy."

"Didn't know you had a son, Buck."

"Doesn't live here most of the time. And don't worry. You ain't gonna see him 'round here any time soon." He turned his back on Cooper and stalked back inside.

5

"BILLY! WAKE UP!"

Billy flipped over and saw a shadowy figure wavering, back-lit by the sun's rays pouring through the mouth of the shallow cave. Unable to determine the identity of the human presence thanks to a lingering alcoholic haze, he panicked. He pushed himself up, then screamed in pain. A broken bottle of Jack Daniel's left a three-inch shard sticking in his palm. "Shit!" He grabbed his hand, eyeing Ray Eddy as the boy knelt at his side. "Fucking asshole."

"Sorry, Billy. Didn't mean to scare ya."

"You don't fucking scare me, you little prick." Billy stared at the jagged piece of glass, gritted his teeth, and yanked the shard out of his hand. Bright red blood flowed freely. He saw the bottom of the bottle, which still held an inch or so of amber liquid, and though the smell nauseated him, he poured the whiskey into the wound. He swallowed the stinging pain, then reached for Buck's best hunting knife. "Hold out the bottom of your shirt!"

"Jesus, Billy!"

"Just hold it, dickbreath. I only got one hand here. Wouldn't want to slip and cut you."

A menacing grin split Billy's face as Ray grasped the bottom edge of his T-shirt and held on tight, afraid to move. He said nothing as Billy sliced a strip of fabric from the bottom of the shirt, blade edging dangerously close to skin, and then watched as Billy wrapped the material around the bleeding wound. When he finished, Ray sank to the ground.

"Why'd ya have to go and do that?"

"It's only a fucking T-shirt, Ray. I got a bunch in the car. An inheritance from old Buck. Go get one."

Ray eyed his friend with concern from under long, stringy bangs. "He'll kill ya, Billy."

"Nah, he'll never catch me. Anyway, I ain't goin' back. I got what I came for." He remembered the two brown boxes in the trunk. "Cleanin' out Buck was just a bonus."

"What are you gonna do now?"

Billy ignored the question. His stomach rumbled, reminding him that, aside from the Jack Daniel's and some homegrown weed, he'd consumed nothing the night before. He rose, steadied himself, and stepped slowly toward the mouth of the cave. Ray stared at the ground.

"Come on! Give me a hand," Billy called as he disappeared into the sunlight.

Ray smiled. "Sure, Billy. Sure."

After a breakfast of cherry Pop-Tarts and Coke, courtesy of Buck, the boys sat in the warm dirt outside the cave and stared at the two cardboard boxes. They were labeled 1 and 2 and had been bound tightly with clear packing tape.

"Open them," Ray said like a child at Christmas. He held up one hand to shield his eyes from the morning sun.

Billy peeled the tape away from the box marked 1. After lifting the flaps, he found a white envelope addressed with his name. A quick glance at the contents of the container revealed nothing but old magazines. Billy tried to hide his disappointment as he ripped open the envelope. Inside, in tiny, neat handwriting, was the following:

Dear Billy,

I was hopin to see you again. But it dont look like I will. Try and forgive your Daddy. Hes a mean man. But hes my son. I'm sure sorry for the way he treated you. But I told him not to marry no woman whos half spic. Not surprisin she run off like she did.

Anyway, its not your fault. I wish I coulda done more for you but I hope this will help some. Could a had more for you if that nigger boss hadn't run me off my job. Never did get that Southern Pacific gold watch. Oh well. By the time you get this I'll be somewhere I don't need no watch.

Stay away from your Daddy boy.

Love,

Grandpa

PS

Ha. Ha. I knew your daddy never would look in a magazine.

"What's it say?" Ray asked.

Billy read the letter out loud, omitting the line about his mother being part Mexican. Nobody needed to know about that. When he finished, he put the letter on the ground beside him and rubbed the top of his head with both hands.

"Why'd your grandpa get fired from the railroad?"

"Shit! What are ya, stupid? Niggers and spics get all the jobs now. Grandpa got run off cause he's white."

Billy looked out over the simmering valley floor below. His grandfather had been a drunk. He knew the old man got caught drinking on the job numerous times. After thirty-two years with the railroad, he'd been fired. Four months later he died.

Billy reached into the box. The Spring 1995 issue of *SP Trainline* rested on top of the pile. Why would his grandfather have left word for him to come all the way from L.A. for a bunch of old magazines? He rummaged through the carton. All of the magazines appeared to be about trains.

Ray grabbed one and began flipping through the pages. "Hey, look at this."

Billy glanced up to see Ray holding a twenty-dollar bill. "Give me that!" Billy reached for the money, dropping the magazine he was holding in the process.

"Look!" Ray pointed to the ground. Another twenty-dollar bill lay in the dirt.

Both boys grabbed for the box and began pulling out magazines. In each one they found a single bill. When all the money had been counted and neatly piled on the ground, Billy's inheritance added up to $1,840.

"I'm fucking rich, Ray!" Billy leaned back against a warm slab of rock.

A sudden wind buffeted the side of the mountain, lifting bills into the air, sending the boys scrambling to gather them up. When they were all collected and safely hidden in the trunk of the blue Chevy, Billy headed for the second box.

"More magazines?" Ray grinned at the prospect.

Billy didn't answer as he peeled back the lid. This container, much heavier than the first, held no magazines. Instead, Billy found a collection of tools, each bearing the Southern Pacific Railroad stamp. He didn't know what most of them were, but he knew his grandfather had taken great pride in his equipment.

Billy removed each tool and lined them up on the ground. Then he found a box which was made of corrugated cardboard, the red and black lettering faded, almost impossible to decipher. But Billy didn't need to read the print to know what was inside. Though he was almost eighteen, he could still appreciate what he knew was a child's toy. His grandfather had left him the old train set, the one with all the little passengers inside, a tiny engineer at the helm, a conductor in his cap and uniform holding a miniscule lantern standing at the rear of the caboose. The Southern Pacific Railroad logo was stamped in gold letters on the side of each car.

"That's cool, Billy." Ray reached for the engine.

"Don't touch it!" Billy snapped as he slipped the cars back into the box.

6

EARLY MORNING SUNLIGHT pushed through the bedroom window, striking the bare wooden floor in a square shaft. Dust danced throughout the sunbeam, mesmerizing Ramm until he felt a wet nose nudging his hand. He rubbed his head and tried to clear away the images that plagued him. The burning boy was just one of many. The dog placed one paw and her muzzle on the bed, gazing at him with soft, adoring eyes.

"Okay, Dog. Just give me a minute." Ramm stroked the animal's head, threw back the covers, and hauled his long naked body out of bed.

Half an hour later, he sat outside eating a peanut butter and grated carrot sandwich. The now empty prescription container taunted him from the tabletop. He'd been cutting the dosage, weaning himself from the powerful medication, and now the pills were gone. He wanted to believe he'd be fine without the drugs. His only other option was to find a hospital. But his former employer was, no doubt, still looking for him and, even if he assumed a different identity, there was the chance he might reveal himself when the images took hold. His mind could betray him and make him a liability. As miserable as he was, he didn't want to die. Not yet.

Ramm took another bite and then, having lost his appetite, gave the rest to Dog. He didn't know how angry his handlers were about the mission's failure. He never checked in when he returned. He just disappeared. If they knew about his stay at Kfar Shaul and the reason for his confinement at the hospital, there was a good possibility they wouldn't want him back. They might even feel the need to have him eliminated.

A soft whinny came from around the side of the house.

"Damn it!" Ramm jumped up, wiped his hands on his jeans, and headed for the horse. "Sorry, Becky." He dropped some hay over the fence and scooped the last of the molasses-flavored grain into the red plastic bucket mounted by the gatepost. "I ordered your feed yesterday, and I'll pick it up for you this afternoon. Gotta run errands, anyway." Ramm still had the groceries he'd picked up for the Children of Light, and they expected the delivery this morning. He scratched the Appaloosa between the ears. "And, maybe, I'll get you some carrots, too."

An hour later, Ramm parked his truck on the gravel drive fronting the main building of the compound owned by the Children of Light.

"Elect Sun?" He tapped on the small pane set high in the front door.

A scholarly looking, seventy-year-old man appeared. "Jason. Please, come in."

"Thank you, Elect Peter." Ramm nodded, as always, taking care to be especially polite to the members of the Children of Light.

"Let me help you with those." Elect Peter bent his wispy frame to lift one of the boxes Ramm had stacked on the porch.

"Elect Sun," Elect Peter called as the two men passed through the communal dining room and into the kitchen. "Jason is here."

A bright smile lit Elect Sun's pale eyes as she nodded in greeting. Wavy gray hair reached below the woman's shoulders. Wearing no make-up, her face reflected her sixty-four years in a glorious array of wrinkles, the byproduct of a life in the desert sun.

"Ma'am." Ramm removed his cowboy hat.

The two commune members put the first of the supplies away, while Ramm toted the rest of the boxes in from the porch.

"Sit, Jason. I'll fix you a glass of lemonade." Elect Sun reached for a chipped red bowl overflowing with lemons. "We picked them this morning." She smiled as Ramm folded his body into one of the green wooden kitchen chairs. "Your father..." She trailed off. "He always loved fresh-squeezed lemonade."

The boy, thirteen, peered up at the handmade wooden sign from the backseat of his father's rusting station wagon: a painted yellow setting sun emitted rays ending in a rainbow, a lush garden surrounded by desert landscape was overlaid with the words Children of Light—on Land of God's Ownership.

The Reverend Alexander Ramm, his car rattling, small stones crunching beneath worn tires, drove down the dusty, date palm-lined lane whistling an old hymn. The people he and his son found at the end of the road were much like themselves— devout Pentecostals—though the Children of Light were descended from a Canadian branch of the faith.

Jason Ramm, the only child in the compound, was doted on from the moment they arrived, and was, at first, overwhelmed by the Children and the attention they lavished on him. The people, gentle and kind, hoped Jason and his father would stay, learn to live their way. The style in which they believed Jesus Christ had lived: "wholly under Spirit control for food, drink, and raiment, selling all worldly possessions, having all in common, forsaking all flesh relations, and living as eunuchs and virgins for the Kingdom of Heaven's sake."

Alexander Ramm, however, was an itinerant preacher, a man who spoke the word of God to housewives and migrant workers, anyone looking for religion, and yes, a little entertainment. Alexander was an amiable, handsome man, and though he understood the choices the Children made, theirs was not a life he'd be content living. He enjoyed the road and the people and the laughter he sometimes coaxed from the lost and lonely. Humor was a gift from God, as was his gregarious personality, both of which would be wasted at the commune.

One year later, Alexander and Jason said good-bye to the Children of Light. The people cried openly and waved as the car clattered down the palm-lined lane back into the world. Jason had turned away from his father, not wanting to show his tears.

The boy had never known his mother, but Elect Sun had given him a glimpse of what having one might have been like. He would miss her the most.

"Jason. Jason. Are you all right?" Elect Sun was holding out a tall glass of lemonade, a worried look on her weathered face.

"Oh. Um. Yes, I'm fine," Ramm said, trying to clear his head.

Elect Sun peered at him like a mother having caught her child in a lie, but she asked no more, and set the glass on the table before him.

"Thank you." Ramm sipped the cool drink, savoring the tart, mildly sweet concoction, just about the perfect desert drink.

A tiny ancient woman entered the room using a walker. Cataracts clouded her eyes. "Jason. I know you're here." She smiled as she inched her way toward the table. He pushed his chair out and began to rise, but she stopped him. "No. No. You sit. I'll get there."

Elect Sarah was blind, yet she seemed to see things with perfect clarity. Did she see through his lies? Would she be making her slow walk toward him, a march ending with a smile and a kiss on his rough cheek, if she really knew him? Would he be forgiven, despite the Children's abhorrence of any form of violence? They were vehement conscientious objectors. By their way of thinking, Ramm's entire adult life was nothing but one long grievous sin. He wanted forgiveness, but knew he was undeserving. Pentecostals believed that God forgave anything. All you had to do was ask. But Ramm couldn't even do that.

Elect Sarah did not have to bend down, just forward a bit, to kiss Ramm on the cheek. She giggled like a young girl. Elect Sun rolled her eyes.

The kitchen door slammed.

"Kelly," Elect Sun called. "Remember about the door."

"Yes, ma'am."

Ramm had not seen the girl's face clearly before. He looked directly at her as she entered the room, and though his face betrayed no hint of the shock most people conveyed when seeing her for the first time, Kelly turned her face down.

"Kelly. Look at me," Elect Sun admonished her. The girl continued to stare at her bare feet. Elect Sun walked over and gently lifted Kelly's chin. "God made you the way you are. God makes nothing that is bad or ugly. You have no reason to be ashamed. This is Mr. Ramm. He is a friend to all of us here. You may call him Jason, if you like." Elect Sun smiled down at her.

Kelly took a breath, then turned and faced Ramm.

Elect Peter spoke. "Kelly was born with what they call Moebius Syndrome."

Ramm pulled his eyes away from the girl, focusing on the elderly man.

"You may remember that before I came here I was a doctor with a family practice. When I met Kelly, I checked up on her condition. It's a very rare birth defect."

"Is there any treatment available?" Ramm asked, smiling at Kelly.

"There are a few surgeons working on repairing some of the facial deformities." Elect Peter placed his arm across Kelly's shoulders.

"Do they know what causes it?"

"It's all rather technical," the doctor said.

"I have some medical knowledge." Ramm flashed back on his required Special Forces training as a medic, and on the number of times he'd seen skulls laid open, bare muscle and tissue exposed.

"Well, it's a defect caused by the absence or underdevelopment of the sixth and seventh cranial nerves. These control horizontal eye movement and all of the facial muscles. Also, the muscles in the lower jaw are affected. Though many with the defect are afflicted with deformed hands, clubbed feet and crossed eyes, as you can see, Kelly is not."

Ramm looked back at the expressionless girl. Her oddly blue eyes stared straight into his. He sensed a familiarity, but didn't know why. Then the sensation passed.

Elect Sun continued. "The only thing Kelly can't do, Jason, is smile."

Ramm's gaze inadvertently slipped from the girl's face to her belly.

"And soon, we will have a gift from God." Elect Sun stroked Kelly's long, blue-black hair.

7

THE SUBTLE AROMA of split pea soup tempted Kelly, but Elect Sun was not finished with the evening blessing, so the girl kept her hands clasped tightly above her belly.

"Amen," Elect Sun ended the prayer.

"Amen," the ten other commune members answered in unison.

A basket containing fresh hot bread was passed around the communal table. The simple meal consisted of soup, bread, and sweet dates, and while this minimal repast suited the older people, Kelly—eight months pregnant and a growing teenager—always found herself hungry, despite the fact that the Children encouraged her to take multiple helpings.

"Kelly needs some protein and more calcium." Elect Peter smiled at the girl.

The Children were vegetarians, strict in the sense that they refused to eat animal flesh. They did, however, allow the consumption of dairy products.

"It will be a while before the cheese is ready." Elect Sun was a master at making the *fromages de chevre* she produced courtesy of the commune's four goats.

"I think we should purchase some." Elect Peter wiped his mouth on a blue cotton napkin.

Elect Sun frowned. The Children enjoyed the belief that they were self-sufficient. Though they had no qualms about accepting outside food donations, they rarely purchased items they could produce themselves.

She watched Kelly devour her soup. "You're right, Peter. We'll get some cheese."

"And some milk. It's a pity we don't have any spinach in the garden right now. That would be a good source of calcium."

If Kelly could have made a face, she would have. She didn't like spinach.

"I'll speak with Jason." Elect Sun turned to Kelly. "By the way, what did you think of our guest today?"

The girl hesitated. She still wasn't used to speaking to anyone but her mother and stepfather. Because of her deformity, her voice had an odd quality that had often drawn as much ridicule as her face. In fact, the combination of her appearance, her speech, and a lack of formal education made people assume she was mentally handicapped. But there was nothing wrong with Kelly's mind. She could learn if her mother had allowed her to, but Miranda Kelly insisted school was out of the question for her only child. The special needs facility was too far away and too expensive, her mother said, so Kelly had remained year-round in her tiny home outside of Agua Caliente where she cooked and cleaned, an arrangement that suited her mother, that is, until recently.

"Kelly," Elect Sun addressed the girl again. "Mr. Ramm. Jason. What did you think of him?"

"Um, I think he's sad."

"Why do you say that?" Elect Sun spooned the last of the soup into Kelly's bowl.

But before Kelly could answer there was a knock at the door. The girl was relieved, but not for long. Elect Peter stood and opened the door that lead onto the screened-in porch. A man with a broad handsome face espousing his Hispanic and Native American heritage stood holding a black cowboy hat close to his chest.

"I'd like to see Kelly." His voice was a barely audible whisper.

Before Elect Peter could respond, Elect Sun was at the door. "I don't think that would be wise, Mr. Garcia."

Eduardo Garcia straightened his back and spoke up. "You cannot keep me away—" He stopped when he heard the tires screech to a halt on the pebbled drive. A car door opened, then slammed shut. Footsteps came fast and deliberate, crunching on the stones. The outside screen door opened. Miranda Garcia, on the porch now, stood ten feet from her husband, hands on her shapely hips. She was out of breath. Loose, jet-black hair, the color of her daughter's, cascaded wildly past her shoulders. Brown eyes framed by long curly lashes pierced Eduardo. Then, from the full soft lips that so many men openly admired, came the venom.

"I told you to stay away from her, you pig!"

"But, Miranda, I have a right …"

"You have no rights!"

"She is my daughter." He nervously rolled the hat, turning the brim in his hands.

"Thank God she's not!" Miranda moved toward him.

Eduardo, embarrassed that these other people were

watching, straightened up. "I supported you both after Bryan killed himself."

Miranda spit on the floor at his feet. "And do you want me to go to the police? Tell them what you've done to your little chica?"

Eduardo moved toward his wife barely concealing his anger.

"Stop!" Elect Sun strained to keep her voice even. "Mrs. Garcia, you asked us to take Kelly in, and we did." She turned to the child. "Kelly, come here, please."

The girl remained rooted to the chair, elbows on the table, hands covering her ears. Elect Peter walked over and gently helped her up. He smiled reassuringly and grasped Kelly's hand as he led her to the door.

"You see," Elect Sun continued. "Kelly is fine and happy here. Am I right, child?"

Kelly nodded but refused to look at her mother or stepfather.

"Kelly," Eduardo stepped toward her.

"Stay away from the brat!" Miranda hissed. "If I ever see you near her again, I'll cut off your balls and stuff them in your mouth."

"That is enough, Mrs. Garcia!" Elect Sun verged on losing her composure. "This is a house of God. We do not talk this way, nor do we abide people who do."

Miranda raised her chin defiantly and looked at Elect Sun. "I'm not afraid of you or God or this shithead I married." She turned to her husband and pointed a long, scarlet fingernail back toward the door. "Go home, Eduardo."

He hesitated briefly, then edged warily past his wife. Miranda, arms folded across her chest, stared at Kelly for a moment, then turned to Elect Sun. "If my husband comes here again, you have my permission to call the police. Make sure they know he was fucking his own retarded step-daughter."

ψ

Kelly sat on the blue and white log cabin-pattern quilt that covered the twin bed and braided her hair. A simple three-drawer dresser, a nightstand, and a blue ceramic lamp with a flowered shade filled the tiny corner room. Above the bed hung a print of Jesus surrounded by animals and adoring children, none of whom, she noted, had a face like hers.

Kelly's favorite part of the room was the four-paned window. From the second floor, she could see past the date palms and the gardens to the stark wild desert beyond. She lifted the window, wanting to hear the soothing night sounds. Crickets chirped their staccato chorus. A far-off coyote howled. Other desert dogs joined his plaintive cry, their sonorous song drifting on the evening air. She smelled burning mesquite from a campfire and the earthy aroma of creosote bushes near the wash. The red-tailed hawk that nested in a nearby cottonwood darted past, a mouse limp in its beak. For a moment, Kelly mourned the tiny creature, but when her tears fell, they were not for the rodent.

8

RAMM SCRAPED THE LAST bit of mortar from the bucket and smoothed the mixture onto the brick. He'd have to get down to the wash and gather more sand if he wanted to finish the fireplace today. After he positioned the brick using the grid line, he troweled off the excess mortar and leaned back to survey his work.

The old bricks he'd collected from the Rowley Mine's dilapidated buildings, weathered and faded, were much more attractive than new ones. Perhaps old Mrs. Rowley would be pleased. Ramm had done some research on the abandoned mine before purchasing the land and found the original owner's wife to be one tough pioneer. She had camped and prospected in the Sonoran Desert wilderness, often alone, with nothing but her Winchester rifle to keep her company. She was tall, strong, and formidable—some might say ornery—and had married a man renowned for his sense of humor.

Ramm pictured the lanky woman, sweating and cursing alongside the men, digging holes in the earth in the hope of becoming rich, probably not realizing that even with money she'd probably never fit in with the well-to-do ladies of her time. He tried to imagine Mrs. Rowley associating with the upper-crust women in feathers and silks and tiny ludicrous hats, sipping tea from wafer-thin cups while they commented on the weather.

He stood and looked around the cozy cabin he'd built, then gazed out the picture window that faced the valley and mountains beyond and which nightly framed magnificent desert sunsets. He removed his gloves and rubbed his damaged shoulder. His knee throbbed. The doctors hadn't been able to piece him back together properly after he'd been blown into the side of an abandoned tank when the soldier ahead of him tripped a landmine.

No matter. He'd been through worse.

He finished his bottle of water and headed down to the wash, just a ten-minute hike from the cabin's front door. As usual these days, Dog accompanied him. While her cuts were healing, she still limped on the broken front leg, but she needed exercise, and the sandy wash provided gentle footing.

Ramm followed the rambling path of the dry stream bed, which with astonishing speed could turn into a raging, deadly torrent during the summer monsoon. He stopped at the foot of a massive pile of tailings, remnants of the mining industry's search for copper and lead, one that, in this case, ended as a losing proposition.

Sand spread out around the base of the rocks, fine grained and so white it sparkled when it slipped through his fingers. A definite oddity for the area. He began filling the green canvas backpack. Ten pounds of sand, when mixed with cement and water, would produce more than enough mortar to finish the fireplace.

Behind him, Dog barked, then began to whine and wag her mottled tail. Ramm stepped around the rock pile and spied her quarry. A long-legged, speckled roadrunner darted back and forth in the wash. Not wanting Dog to run hard on her injured leg, he reached down and took hold of the bright red collar, purchased in the hope it might stop an overzealous farmer from mistaking her for a feral beast, a mistake which could easily leave the dog a victim of a bullet.

He tossed a pebble at the bird, and the roadrunner scrambled up and out of the wash and into the open desert. He knelt and held the dog tightly, talking to her, stroking her until the bird was out of sight. When the dog stopped fidgeting, Ramm gave her a treat from his pocket, released her, and returned to the knapsack.

After he'd collected enough sand, he buckled the canvas straps and attempted to stand, but a stabbing pain in his forehead caused him to drop cross-legged to the ground. Ramm forced himself to breathe deeply, steadily, and then tried again to rise, but the sunlight reflecting off the sand pierced his brain, and the pain sharpened. He looked around, crawled several yards into the meager shade of a palo verde tree, pulled his hat down over his eyes, and waited for the pain to pass.

He stood on the brilliant white sand, strong, tall, invincible: one of hundreds of soldiers playing at war, practicing for the real thing. They'd be shipped out any day to a war that raged in swamps and jungle, yet they rehearsed here, on a sandy New Mexico beach with no water in sight.

Before he set foot on foreign soil to take part in the bitter war that changed his life forever, he saw his first man die. The war games at White Sands were a teaching tool, but that day the games had gone awry. Live ammunition was used, but as the sergeant pointed out, "If you keep your fucking heads down, the machine gunfire can't get you."

The members of his unit listened and understood and, rifles in hand, crawled on their bellies toward the machine guns they were expected to capture. Just an unfortunate accident was the explanation that came later. A bolt had slipped, allowing one of the guns to drop down, which eliminated the safety zone the soldiers had been counting on.

Sammy Ratigliano, of Bayonne, New Jersey, was the first one hit. The boy's head burst open with a crack, depositing gray brain tissue on the soldiers behind him. The black kid from Georgia was shot next, grasping at his neck, suffocating in his own blood before a second bullet ended his agony. White sand kicked up. Bullets thunked into flesh. Screams permeated the air, but the shooter was too far away, oblivious to the mistake and the devastation and the wailing of the boys not long out of high school, most of whom had never been away from home, and now would never be anywhere but in their grieving relatives' minds.

A bullet struck nearby and deflected a sharp piece of stone or metal; he would never know which. He felt a piercing pain as the top knuckle on his left pinkie was amputated. Blood and tears streamed into the sand. He stood, threw his rifle to the ground, and ran.

Ramm felt warm blood on his face. No, he was wrong. His face was wet, but when he opened his eyes he saw Dog patiently licking him. There was no blood; there were no bodies. The sand sparkled in the sunlight and, above him, he saw the cool, clean blue of the desert sky, and a hawk gliding effortlessly on the currents.

The sun had shifted. Ramm lay in a shadow cast by the tailings. He sat up slowly. He'd gripped fistfuls of white sand so tightly that moving his hands was agony. He rubbed them hard to work the blood back. Seeing the amputated appendage, he felt like laughing at the absurdity of the wound. Fifteen soldiers died that day, and Ramm wondered, not for the first time, how much better off he might have been had he died on the white sands of New Mexico with them.

9

BILLY EASED THE RUSTED Chevy to a halt in front of the dirt drive that led to his father's mobile home. He took another draught from the can of Bud, and considered again whether he should torch the place. There wasn't another building in sight, so he knew he could get away without being seen. He grinned at the thought of Buck having to sleep on that pile of worm-eaten burlap sacks in the back room at the station, the same place he'd periodically locked Billy for any number of transgressions over the years. There was no heat or air conditioning in the dank space, just one small high window and little light. The place smelled of cat piss and rodent droppings. Termites squirmed in the walls. Billy remembered peeling the rotten wood away, and watching the tiny white larva writhe in protest when exposed.

He drained the last of the beer, tossed the can out the window, and glanced at the rearview mirror. A plume of dust rose down the road.

"Shit!" The red and blue panel of lights topping the vehicle were now clearly visible. Billy slammed the car into reverse and caught sight of Buck's mailbox. He smiled.

Anything he could do to screw up his father's existence was worth the effort. He cleaned out the box and tossed the mail in the backseat of the Chevy.

Later, Billy reclined in the camouflage-colored canvas folding chair Buck had purchased for relaxing around the campfire after a day of hunting. Lazily intoxicated, mildly content, he stretched his legs, and turned his face to the sun.

The cave behind him was cluttered with Buck's possessions, including enough provisions to allow Billy to stay there comfortably for about a month. With his grandfather's money, there was no telling how long he could hold out.

Billy was jolted from his reverie by a rustling sound. He lifted the Smith & Wesson .380 he'd stolen from Buck, but his view was hazy due to the twelve-pack he'd consumed. He expected to see a jackrabbit or a bird or maybe a red fox, something to give him a little competition, so the lumbering desert tortoise that crawled out from under a scraggly, sprawling prickly pear proved a disappointment.

The animal, which seemed not to notice Billy, plodded along at a leisurely pace. The tortoise propelled itself forward in a slow-motion ballet, then stopped for an instant, one leg poised in the air, leathered head turned as if contemplating something disconcerting.

Billy had to squint to focus, but he still managed to blow the tortoise's head off with the first shot. He emptied the clip into the reptile's shell.

Ray arrived a few hours later and found Billy absorbed in a magazine and surrounded by a scattering of unpaid bills and junk mail. Hitting a slick spot on the ground, he slipped.

"Shit! What the hell!?" Ray regained his balance. "What's this?" He inspected a gooey mess that clung to the bottom of one Reebok.

"Turtle head," Billy said, glancing at the dangling gunk.

Ray scraped the sole of his shoe with a rock. He spied the empty cans littering the ground. "Got any left?"

"In the cooler," Billy answered without lifting his head.

The snap and fizz of a pop-top followed. Ray walked over to the oozing tortoise shell that was already being devoured by both crawling and flying insects and from which a noxious odor was emanating. He toed the mess over the side of the hill then sat on the ground at Billy's feet. He scraped again at the flesh that remained in the indentations on the sole of his shoe.

"It's perfect."

"What?" Ray tossed the gummy rock away.

"The train. I know I can do it. All the directions are right here. It'll be just like bakin' a cake."

"I didn't know you could bake."

"For God's sake, Ray. You really are as dumb as you look. I ain't talkin' about bakin' anything. I'm talkin' about derailing a train. It's all right here!" He thumped the magazine in his lap.

"What is?"

"Check it out. I lifted it from Buck's mailbox." Billy tossed the magazine at Ray. *"SP Trainline.* It's addressed to my granddaddy. Shitheads don't even know he's dead, I guess."

"This the same magazine that had the money in it?"

"Yeah. Here." Billy reached over, grabbed the magazine from Ray and flipped through the pages. "Right here. This article." Billy jabbed his index finger into the page.

Ray stared straight ahead.

"Damn! I forgot. Little Ray-Ray can't read." Billy rolled his eyes. "Well, I guess I'll just have to tell you about it. Goes like this. There was a train wreck in 1939."

"What's that got to do with us?"

"Just shut up and listen. Somebody derailed a train near Harney, Nevada. Loosened a rail on a curve before a bridge. They even ran a wire to make sure the engineer never got a signal that the track was broken. Twenty-four people were killed." Billy smiled.

Ray was frightened by the look on his friend's face, but said nothing.

"The Feds still don't know who did it. It's a perfect crime. And if we can kill more people, our crime will be even better."

"But ... but Billy ..."

"Oh, Ray. Just shut up and let me do the thinking."

"We don't know how to derail no train."

"Sure we do," Billy ripped the magazine from Ray's hands. "It's right here in black and white. Shows exactly how they did it. See. Look at the pictures. It even tells what tools they used. And, wouldn't you know, my granddaddy left me everything we'll need. I'll be fucking famous."

Billy leaned back in the chair. "Get me a cold one, Ray." He wished some of his friends back in L.A. were here. The crimes they were so proud of committing, the ones they pulled to join the Aryan Brotherhood, to gain respect in the gang, were so piddling compared to wrecking a fucking train.

"First we need to pick just the right spot."

10

RAMM SCREAMED. The dreams were back. Not that they had ever left him completely. Drugs muddied up the visions, blurred the edges, and dulled their brightness like the faded color on an old television. Medication made the nightmares almost bearable. But the pills were gone.

Dog sniffed at the sweat-soaked sheets. Ramm eased himself from the bed. Any further attempt at sleep was futile, and, despite the fact that the sun would not rise for at least another hour, he stripped the sheets, dropping them to the floor, and headed for the shower.

Ramm stepped into the steaming stream of water and scalded his back to release the tension in his aching muscles. He let the water beat on the ragged scar that ran the length of his thigh. He touched the old wound. But for the South Vietnamese lieutenant—a soldier Ramm had trained when he wore a red beret and held the title advisor somewhere in the wilderness on the Cambodian border— he would be dead. In fact, he had been listed as such, and his father notified that he had been Killed in Action.

Lu had located Ramm at the bottom of a pile of mutilated American and South Vietnamese corpses: the VC had removed ears and testicles and other parts for trophies. Though the butchers passed him over, the bullets had severed the main artery in his thigh. The doctors and nurses who tended him in Saigon were amazed when he woke up four weeks later, stunned that he hadn't bled to death in that pile of human meat. He asked to call home and found that his father had died seven days earlier, the grief of losing his son in the war too much for him to bear. Ramm had given instructions for his father's burial and, having no one to go home to, re-upped for a second tour.

Dressed in worn jeans and a soft, faded flannel shirt, Ramm put the kettle on the stove. He slumped into a hard-backed pine chair and stroked Dog's head.

Ψ

Two hours later, the sun was bright on the eastern horizon. Ramm turned his truck down the dirt road leading to what was left of the Hotel Modesti. The structure had been built around the turn of the twentieth century and was situated next to a natural hot spring that once bubbled up at an almost constant 118 degrees. The spring, noted for a multitude of healing minerals, drew visitors from all over the country. Even President Teddy Roosevelt had come to take the waters. But in the late 1950s, drilling to provide irrigation for farmland in the lower Gila River Valley destroyed the spring and aquifer, and people stopped coming.

The old hotel, desolate and boarded-up, crumbled as the desert slowly reclaimed the building. Ramm could see the structure in the distance, but as he approached the Agua Caliente Pioneer Cemetery, he made an unscheduled stop.

He saw her sitting among the headstones. An odd tune drifted on the warm morning breeze. He did not understand the words, but the overall effect was light and rhythmic, more chant than song. The sound drifted in and out on the shifting wind that came from the planted fields below and rebounded from the black basalt mountain that rose across the road.

Ramm stepped out of the truck and walked over to the cemetery's low stone wall that was built from the rhyolite, quartz, and the dark basalt that littered the region. He lifted the bent wire that secured the gate, pushed the door open, and entered.

The girl's shiny black hair moved back and forth as she swayed with the song. Ramm walked slowly, not wanting to frighten her. He passed timeworn headstones: Geronimo Cruz 1856-1916, Lee R. Bailey 1894-1966, and Steven Duane Eddy 1952-1974. His foot crunched on the gravel.

The girl whirled around.

"Kelly," Ramm said in a gentle voice.

She didn't answer and turned her face toward the barking.

"No! Stay!" Ramm called, worried that a jump from the pickup's window might reinjure the dog's leg. But the animal ignored him and leaped from the truck. She jumped awkwardly over the stone wall and limped toward them. Ramm grabbed her just before she got to Kelly. "Bad girl!"

Dog wagged her tail and whined, straining toward Kelly. "She won't hurt you," Ramm said, though Kelly didn't seem the least bit afraid. "Would you like to meet her? Her name is Dog."

Kelly nodded and Ramm released his hold. Dog bounded over and licked the girl's face. Kelly smoothed the fur on the dog's rump and the animal sat down, tongue lolling out of the side of her mouth.

Ramm focused on the smooth pink granite stone at Kelly's feet. It read: Bryan Kelly Gone But Not Forgotten. The shape of a Purple Heart was etched into the stone.

Kelly saw him looking at the grave marker. "My father," she explained in her odd guttural tone. The dog was now lying with her head in Kelly's lap.

Ramm looked at Kelly, careful not to react to her mask-like expression, which no doubt made others stare and whisper and point and laugh.

He sat on the ground. Only a droning horsefly and dry desert air passed between them. Ramm scanned the dilapidated cemetery, some grave markers flat and relatively new, like Bryan Kelly's, others nothing more than crude metal crosses on which names and dates were crookedly carved. His gaze fixed on a spot where sprigs of bright red bougainvillea had been placed. He noticed many more fresh blooms on several graves clustered closely together.

"The flowers are for the babies," she said. "The little ones who died a long time ago. When I come to see my father, I visit them, too."

Ramm could think of nothing to say and was surprised when Kelly continued the conversation.

"My mother doesn't want me anymore," she said matter-of-factly, not a hint of self-pity in her voice. "Did your mother want you?"

He thought for a moment. Then he lied. "She died when I was very young. I hardly remember her."

51

"And your father?"

Ramm hesitated and turned away from the girl. "He was a preacher."

"What kind?"

"Pentecostal. Like the Children." Ramm quickly changed the subject. "How is school?"

Kelly shook her head. The words rushed out. "I've never been to school. My mother says I'm too dumb. She says the other kids will just laugh at me, call me stupid, and make fun of my face, and the way I talk." She struggled to her feet before he had a chance to respond. Ramm reached over to help, but she pushed herself up without his assistance. "I have to get back."

Ramm stood and watched her move slowly toward the gate. Then Kelly hesitated a moment, changed direction, and walked to the eastern wall of the cemetery where she stopped at the grave in the corner. Ramm joined her and they both stood looking down at the white marble headstone that marked the grave of Alexander Ramm.

Several hours later, Ramm slowed to a stop, his breath coming in gasps, his heart pounding in protest. He had recently avoided any sustained aerobic exercise, and now paid the price. He leaned forward, hands on his thighs, face down at the trail that wound through desert brush and rocky outcroppings. The earthy odor of creosote—a strangely pleasing, moldy scent—wafted from a nearby ravine. The desert air was unusually free of dust, allowing Ramm to see the distant mountains in sharp outline. The vista was dotted with bright green patches, courtesy of regular irrigation, tiny amidst the parched browns of what had once been verdant lowlands bordering a seasonally mighty river.

But the Gila was dead now, sickened by settlers whose wagon trains scored the land, allowing the water to run unabated into the desert, and by the domesticated animals that ate away the riverside foliage, causing erosion. Finally, the Gila was killed by the building of the Roosevelt and Coolidge Dams. With the water gone, the wildlife disappeared. The beaver, deer, waterfowl, and upland game birds all vanished. Only the heartiest and most adaptable living things survived in this land now.

Ramm sipped some water, twisted the cap back on the bottle, and began the run back to the cabin. A tiny emerald hummingbird darted down the path distracting him. Though he had spent most of his youth in a series of small Midwestern towns, he had no trouble appreciating the desert's spare beauty. A stately snow crane glided over one of the iridescent, irrigated fields. Attracted by the bird's graceful flight, Ramm nearly stepped on the coiled reptile. The snake's rattle startled him. He took an awkward step, lost his balance, but managed to right himself. The snake hissed in annoyance, tongue darting in and out. Ramm saw the bulge at the diamondback's midsection. Some rodent was not having a good day. Easing his way around the creature, Ramm continued down the path.

After a shower, he made a bowl of soup and settled at the kitchen table. Dog curled up at his feet, and he smiled at her. Maybe tonight, after the run, he would be able to sleep.

Ramm took a spoonful of soup—homemade black bean and rice that Elect Sun insisted he take in thanks for the supplies. The Children had also given him several loaves of crusty brown bread made from a secret recipe known only to Elect Peter. Ramm sopped up the soup with several pieces of bread, then collected the plates and cleaned the kitchen.

He fed Dog, went outside to check on Becky, and then sat in the overstuffed chair in the living room. The Bible he'd picked up at a second-hand shop in Casa Grande rested in his lap. Ramm ran his hand over the gold lettering on the cover and felt an energy around the book that both compelled and alarmed him. He forced himself not to think about what had happened in Jerusalem, the first time in his life he had been totally out of control, a frightening experience for someone renowned for possessing such cold, exacting skills. Could he lose himself again? Could just touching the book bring on the madness? The empty prescription bottle stared at him from the side table. Ramm opened the book. A crimson ribbon marked the words of Psalm 25.

Do not remember the sins of my youth, nor my transgressions; According to your mercy remember me … Look on my affliction and my pain, And forgive all my sins.

Ramm searched the pages of the Bible until his eyes could no longer focus, then he closed the book, the solace he sought still unattained. In fact, the reverse had happened. His mind was so filled with words that salvation seemed impossible. How did so many others find the help they needed in this book, yet there seemed to be no words in the Bible for him?

He wished he could speak with the burning boy. That was how he thought of him now. Strangely, this was less painful than remembering who the soldier had been before the fire. And the bullet that had mercifully ended his young life.

Ramm closed the book with a simple prayer. *Just let me sleep in peace.*

But Ramm's petition went unanswered. Visions tormented him: the twisting path of the Via Dolorosa; prey caught in his riflescope; the Jerusalem insanity that had seemed so reasonable, so oddly peaceful. Then the face of the girl had appeared. He saw her everywhere he looked, the permanent sadness, a melancholy nothing could heal. She stared at him from paintings and statues, a woman glorified through the ages for her suffering and despair.

11

BIRDS CHIRPED OUTSIDE the open window, but the song they made was supplanted by noise emanating from the kitchen below. Kelly did not open her eyes at first. She had spent her entire life listening to her mother's voice, the tone often etched with anger and disappointment. Poverty, what she perceived as abandonment by Bryan Kelly since he voluntarily joined the army, and the ultimate punishment of bearing an ugly child all conspired to torment Miranda. Though she worked hard to flaunt her own considerable beauty, when others saw Kelly, it detracted from her sense of self worth. And worse, whenever the deformed child became the center of attention, Miranda's pulchritude was swept aside by her homely progeny.

Kelly opened her eyes surprised to find she was not at home, though that was her mother's voice she heard. A door banged below. Kelly rolled onto her side and pushed her body up. She glanced at the clock by the bedside. She'd slept ten hours, still she remained tired. The baby moved.

Kelly slipped on a faded periwinkle sun dress that reached past her knees, then padded shoeless down the stairs and into the kitchen. Elect Sun sat alone at the table, a glass of fresh-squeezed grapefruit juice sitting untouched before her. Kelly walked over and sat at the table, folded her hands neatly in her lap and waited for Miranda to reappear.

"Where is my mother?" she asked after several minutes.

Elect Sun sighed. "Gone. But she wanted me to tell you that she'll be back, and that you should pack your things."

"Where are we going?" Kelly asked, surprised and saddened at the thought of leaving the Children. "I thought I was staying here."

"You're going to Los Angeles. To stay with your mother's sister Lilliana." Elect Sun wrapped her leathered hands around the juice glass, but she didn't drink.

"Who?"

"Your mother's sister?"

"I don't know her."

"Your mother thinks it's for the best."

"How far away is Los Angeles?"

"I'm not really sure," Elect Sun said. "I've never been there."

Kelly rose from the table and walked out the kitchen's back door. She passed Elect Peter who was on his way in, but said nothing when he greeted her. She sat on the steps and listened to her guardians talk.

"There was nothing I could do," Elect Peter lamented when he joined Elect Sun at the table. "The woman would not listen to reason. She has legal custody of the child. Kelly's a minor. You know as well as I do that she wants Kelly away from her husband. As she was leaving, she yelled something about not wanting a brat for Eduardo to dote on, and that she was tired of being ignored in her own house."

"We have no recourse?"

"I'm afraid not. Mrs. Garcia insists that Kelly leave Sunday night. She doesn't want the baby born here or anywhere nearby."

"That's just two days from now." Elect Sun glanced at a calendar tacked to a strip of faded floral wallpaper. Above the dates, the suffering face of a blond Jesus, blood dripping from his crown of thorns, gazed back at her with sorrowful blue eyes. "How will she get to Los Angeles?"

"The train. The Sunset Limited will pass through late Sunday night. Miranda plans to put her on it."

"Alone?"

Elect Peter didn't answer.

Kelly sat on the steps of the abandoned Hotel Modesti, the bleached walls and boarded-up windows shielding ghosts of another time. Across the dirt road was an empty concrete pool built to hold the mineral water that once brought the afflicted to Agua Caliente. Crumbling stone huts dotted the road, constructed for those wishing some privacy as they took the waters searching for a cure.

Kelly tossed a stone, but the pool was too far away, and the pebble clattered off between some rocks and a sprawling prickly pear. She liked to come to the old hotel and imagine that the healing water that had once bubbled out of the ground—and about which the Children had told her—could perform miracles. Like the water priests used on the heads of new babies, which she had been taught to dab on herself in the sign of the cross when her father was living, and she had been allowed to go to church. Back then she'd wanted to splash holy water on her face. If she had, maybe she would look normal now. But she never tried, and now there was no water here, either. There would be no miracle for her.

Los Angeles. All she knew about the city was that they played basketball there. Her stepfather often watched the men in gold shorts run up and down a wood floor, on the television in the living room. He roared with pride whenever the Los Angeles Lakers won a game, a fascination she never understood.

Kelly's mother brought Eduardo home for the first time almost a year after Bryan Kelly killed himself. Miranda had cleaned out the closets. All of her father's clothes were discarded. Kelly begged her mother to let her keep something that had belonged to him, but Miranda refused. Only the Silver Star remained, hidden under Kelly's bed, because she removed the medal from the pile when her mother wasn't looking. When all of Bryan Kelly's things were gone, Miranda went out in her snug-fitting red dress and matching heels, face brightly painted, raven hair long and loose. She was gone every night for several weeks.

Then, Eduardo Garcia appeared with his TV, his suitcase, and his black pickup. Miranda told people they were husband and wife, but Kelly didn't recall a marriage ceremony. At first, she thought they had just neglected to invite her, but later she guessed they probably never really married at all.

Eduardo was nice to Kelly. He didn't act as if her face bothered him, and while he did not go out of his way to spend time with her, initially, he always brought her candy or a small trinket when he had been away. His presence also made Miranda relatively happy so, for a time, things in the tiny house halfway between Hyder and Agua Caliente improved.

As Kelly neared her fifteenth birthday, she sensed a change in Eduardo. His attention confused and sometimes frightened her, his actions varying depending on whether Miranda was home or not. He spent more time talking to her. He bought her more expensive gifts—a small locket, a bottle of perfume, a gold chain—with the caveat that there was no need to mention these trinkets to her mother. Miranda, who had never been very maternal anyway, withdrew even further from her child, criticizing her daughter for the slightest infraction, sending her to the chicken coop to sleep with the birds.

One afternoon when Miranda was at the market, Eduardo asked Kelly to sit beside him on the couch. He smiled, his dark face smooth and handsome. Kelly was too stunned to move when he reached over and ran his fingers down her immobile face. Instinctively, she pulled away, but he spoke to her in a soothing, gentle voice, and coaxed her back to him. Eduardo leaned over and kissed her on the mouth, a stunning display for a girl who had not been touched by another person in anything but anger since her father died. Soon there was a change in Eduardo. He removed Kelly's clothes, urged her to relax and lie on the couch. He stared down at the naked girl and said something Kelly never believed she would ever hear.

"You are beautiful!" Eduardo Garcia exclaimed.

When it became obvious Kelly was pregnant, Miranda threw everything Eduardo owned into the yard. The television landed screen-side down with a thud on the cement-hard caliche. Shards of broken glass glittered like daggers in the harsh sunlight. Chickens scratched at the dry earth around the TV, the electrical cord unfurled like a snake.

Miranda took a broom to Eduardo. She swore and spit like an angry animal. When he jumped inside the truck cab to avoid the blows, Miranda beat on the windshield. After Eduardo drove away, screaming curses in English and Spanish, Miranda turned and used the broom on her daughter.

Kelly assumed having another mouth to feed was the real problem. Miranda always complained about never having enough money, and the child would certainly be an added expense. She had no way of knowing that her behavior with Eduardo was wrong. She had often listened to her parents make love through the thin walls and sensed their happiness. Eduardo produced the same sounds and general sense of satisfaction when he was with Kelly. Wasn't this the way all families behaved?

And there was nothing horribly unpleasant about the attention Eduardo lavished on her. He had only hurt her once, just a little the first time. After that, he had always been gentle and kind, attentive in a way no one had ever been to her before. Since Kelly had so little contact with anyone outside her home, she had no understanding of how others would perceive her behavior with her stepfather. Nor did she realize a baby might start to grow inside her.

After Miranda let Eduardo back into the house, he stayed away from Kelly, but Miranda could not stand to look at her only child. That Eduardo had turned away from her and was attracted to her deformed daughter was simply more than Miranda's considerable ego could bear. After a brief conversation with Elect Sun, the decision was made to send Kelly to live with the Children.

Kelly stared again at the empty pool, bereft of the miracle water that lured the afflicted from far away so many years ago. She felt the baby move, then rose from the warm, white stone steps of the ruined Hotel Modesti and walked toward the compound.

12

THE CHEVY PULLED to a crawl just a few yards behind the girl in the blue sundress. Her hair swung rhythmically as she walked, brown shoulders, arms and legs naked to the sun. Billy James eased the car closer and called out. "Hey, baby, need a ride?"

The girl ignored him.

"Hey! I asked you a question." Kelly quickened her pace.

Billy hated to be ignored. "Hey, bitch!" He pulled the car alongside Kelly and saw her belly. "Woah! Somebody got there first, eh babe?"

Kelly, too pregnant to run, moved as quickly as she could, keeping her eyes down, her face turned away from the boy in the car.

But Billy kept pace. The last time he'd had a piece of ass was that little whore in the neighborhood back home in L.A. She'd followed him around relentlessly, until he told her he'd be her boyfriend if she'd fuck all his friends. Billy did her first, then watched the other boys go at her. Afterward, he laughed and told her to fuck off.

He'd never done a pregnant girl before, not that he knew of anyway. Still, she had a pussy, didn't she? She looked

Mexican or Indian, which to Billy meant nobody would probably give a damn if he played with her a little.

"Come on, chiquita, I know you've done it before. No big deal."

Kelly veered off the road into the desert.

Billy watched the girl, drumming his fingers on the steering wheel. He scanned the area. First, he looked down the road before him, then he checked the rearview mirror. The girl was about fifty yards away across rocky undulating ground. Driving would be problematic. When he determined there wasn't a soul around, Billy felt his dick stiffen. He reached for the door handle.

He quickly covered the distance between them. Billy grabbed her shoulder. She froze. He spun Kelly around and watched her hands jerk up and cover her face.

"I won't hurt you. Just do what I say." He laughed. "Just want a little fun. You know." He poked her belly.

Kelly remained still, her hands and dark hair shielding her face.

"Quit playin' with me, bitch!" Billy grabbed her wrists and wrenched her arms.

"No! Please, don't." Kelly's hair fell back.

Billy blinked, then let go and stepped away. "What's the matter with your face? What are you, retarded or something?"

Kelly said nothing, then raised her chin and refused to look away.

"Jesus, you are *ugly*." Billy paused as he looked her over. Then, the grin returned. "But you know what, babe? This is your lucky day, cause I'm gonna do you anyway."

Unzipping his jeans, Billy reached inside and grabbed

his penis. "See, baby. This here is for you." He put one hand on Kelly's shoulder and pushed her to the ground, slamming her knee into a sharp rock that sliced the skin open. "First a little foreplay. Now open wide." He pushed his dick up against her face.

He never saw the dog.

The animal tore into him from behind, grabbing Billy's calf in her teeth. He screamed and fell sideways, kicking violently, instinctively trying to protect his face from the dog. Kelly, terrified, was unable to move.

"Dog! No! Stop!" Jason Ramm yelled from the roadside.

By the time he reached Kelly, the dog stood snarling, muzzle inches from Billy's head, teeth bared, drool slathering onto his face.

After Ramm did a visual check to see that Kelly was not seriously hurt, he yanked Billy off the ground and then burst out laughing. The boy had rolled into a jumping cholla, the most reviled of desert plants, a cactus noted for fishhook-shaped needles that, once they pierced the skin, were almost impossible to remove. And they had definitely pierced Billy's skin. A thick stem with wicked spines had attached itself to Billy's now flaccid penis.

The kid howled as he tried to pull needles from his groin only to have numerous spines sink into his hands. He would not be messing with the ladies anytime soon.

Ramm grabbed the boy by the collar and yanked him to his feet. "Listen, you fucking little piece of shit," Ramm said under his breath, so Kelly wouldn't hear. "I should kill your sorry ass right here and now, but I'm feeling benevolent." He let go. Billy stumbled back, tripped over the cholla, and fell to the ground. The dog barked and lunged.

"Keep that fucking dog away from me!"

"What the—" The big man grabbed Billy again, yanked him by the arm, and pushed the boy's sleeve up to expose the rest of the jagged swastika tattoo. "Under the circumstances, I should just let the dog kill you. After all, that's what you tried to do to her, isn't it?"

"What? I don't know what you're—" Billy stopped, and looked hard at the snarling animal, ears flat on her head, a low growl emanating from deep in her throat.

"You are one sick motherfucker!" And, despite not wanting to resort to violence in front of the girl, Ramm balled his fist and slammed Billy's face, breaking his nose, splattering gobs of blood on himself and the boy.

Ramm regained his composure and became so icily calm Billy's fear solidified in his gut. "If I ever see you near the girl or the dog again, I will kill you."

Billy eyed the tall, muscular man with the big hands. There was something in the cold blue eyes, something Billy didn't like. The boy scrambled to his feet, and, with one hand protecting his groin and the other holding up his pants, he stumbled toward the car.

13

AFTER KELLY'S WOUNDED KNEE was cleansed, she was examined by Elect Peter for any further injuries, and sent to bed.

Ramm sat with Elect Sun at the kitchen table, his hands wrapped around a sweating glass of iced tea.

"Jason, we have always appreciated the help and kindness you show to us, but we are especially grateful today." Tears slipped down her wrinkled cheeks. "When I think of what might have ..."

"She'll be fine," he answered, uncomfortable taking a compliment, feeling unworthy of Elect Sun's kind words.

His gaze rested upon the bleeding Jesus on the wall calendar. A flash of heat, then a claustrophobic crush seized him. Politely refusing the offer of joining the Children for their evening meal, Ramm excused himself and rushed home.

The run and shower did not help. Images plagued him. The boy. Kelly. Ugly visions of what might have been, had he not driven by.

Ramm breathed deeply to calm himself. Pentecostals, in fact all believers in Jesus, were advised to turn the other cheek. The eye-for-an-eye beliefs of the Old Testament supplanted by the kinder, gentler Christian tenets of the New. Still, Ramm could not forget the words from Exodus.

You shall not afflict any widow or fatherless child.

If you afflict them in any way, and they cry at all to Me, I will surely hear their cry.

And my wrath will become hot, and I will Kill you with the sword …

Ramm paced the living room, ignoring the fiery orange sunset that blazed in the western sky. An edgy discomfort took hold, mimicking an overdose of caffeine. He clenched and unclenched his fists, noting the bruise forming where his hand made contact with the boy's face. Ramm relished the ache. Physical pain he understood.

Popping the kid in the face was not what bothered Ramm. The little shit deserved a broken nose. He'd gotten off easy. If Kelly hadn't been there, Ramm would have … *What would he have done?*

He took another deep breath and let the air out slowly. The fact that he had lost his temper was the problem. Ramm had survived all these years in part because of his unwavering demeanor: the cool, detached perfectionist. He slumped onto the couch, too tired to start a fire, too tired to eat. The skilled operative he'd been for over twenty years hadn't been around for quite some time. He'd lost that man on his last assignment. Somewhere in Jerusalem.

Ramm stared out the window at the multihued Sonoran Desert sky and recalled other sunsets, blazing kaleidoscopic infernos in Vietnam. The killing there had been relatively easy, compared to his later missions. Initially, it was a simple matter of survival: kill or be killed. No justification was necessary. Things changed when he became a sniper. He'd be strapped in a treetop for days or crouched, invisible, immobile, blending in with a rock pile, waiting for his mark to appear.

During the war, his targets were bad people. The enemy. The world would be better off without them. That they were sometimes unarmed and periodically civilians disturbed him, at first, but he followed orders and proved to be extraordinarily skilled at his job. Not only was he an exceptional distance shooter, he had no qualms about striking a target at close range. He killed quickly, quietly, with any number of weapons including his bare hands. He was also smart. His handlers finally learned to just give him the target's background information and known location, and leave the planning to him.

While he found no thrill in the actual killing, Ramm enjoyed the renown of his peers as his reputation grew. And, like others before him, he ended up being too good at what he did. The job came with a built-in shelf life, and he eventually became a target himself. Whenever he entered a crowded area, others stepped away, looking over their shoulders, waiting for a shot to ring out. A sniper sniping a sniper.

His superiors had too much invested in Ramm to lose him in the field, so they had pulled him out of Vietnam and gave him an honorable discharge. In truth, however, he never stopped serving. Like other highly trained special operations veterans, mostly former Army Rangers and Navy Seals, Ramm remained on call with a bag by the door, prepared to leave on a special assignment at a moment's notice. Their credo: *semper paratus*. Always ready.

69

Ramm never questioned the logic behind his assignments and willingly traveled to Libya or Guatemala or Turkey or Iraq or any one of myriad countries where his skills had been needed. Nor did he ever question why his targets deserved to die. He was a good soldier. He did his job well and was paid handsomely.

Now Ramm wondered if he'd been chosen for this work because of something other than his skill with a rifle. Had one of the many personality profiles he'd been subjected to painted him as a man who could perform these tasks without question or remorse? Or could the military mold any average person into a killing machine? Why had he been able to so capably perform his duties for so long without contrition? And why was he no longer able to do so?

How had Jerusalem changed him?

And why?

The target who drew him to the ancient city was an elderly Hasidic Jew. Ramm, as always, was given no information about the man's crime, only his whereabouts and the timeframe in which the hit must occur. Everything about the trip to the center of the Judeo-Christian-Muslim world seemed routine. He posed as an ordinary American tourist eager to see the Church of the Holy Sepulcher, the Via Dolorosa, and the other holy sites that drew Christian pilgrims to the city. He passed through customs at Ben Gurion airport undisguised, albeit with a passport issued under an assumed name.

Ramm easily located the target and followed the man for a few days to learn his habits. He planned a quiet kill, one that hopefully would not be discovered for at least several hours, allowing him an easy escape. He planned to use a common everyday item as a weapon. Or maybe just his hands. He'd performed the task countless times before. The job should have been simple.

14

WITH RESOLUTE DETERMINATION, Elect Sun yanked the scorched weeds and sere residue remaining from the last garden crop. She jerked a tomato plant, wrenching the withered roots from the ground, and tossed the brown stalk onto the mounting pile next to her. She'd been working several hours, and her back ached. She had hoped the arduous manual labor would help her overcome the animosity she felt toward Miranda Garcia, such feelings, she believed, being an affront to God.

She worked her way down the furrowed rows on hands and knees in the surprisingly dark soil, a testament to constant additions from the compost heap by the shed. Despite the hard work, uncharitable thoughts tormented her. Why didn't Miranda understand that the best place for Kelly and her baby was here with the Children? Elect Sun gritted her teeth as she fought a stout desert weed. How could a mother not love her own child?

The crunching of pebbles signaled someone walking up the garden path. The last person Elect Sun expected to see was Miranda. Kelly's mother had a smug look of superiority on her face, one that effectively erased her natural beauty.

"Mrs. Garcia." Elect Sun made a concerted effort to mask her hostility. She did not rise to greet the woman, but continued her way down the row, eliminating the garden detritus.

Miranda tugged something out of the back pocket of her skintight black jeans, and dropped a blank white envelope onto the ground. Elect Sun sighed, sat back on her haunches, and stared up at the woman.

"It's a ticket for the train. It'll be stopping in Hyder at twelve fifty-five Monday morning." Miranda folded her arms defiantly across her prominent chest.

Elect Sun reached for the envelope, then looked inside. "There's only one ticket here. The child is going by herself?"

Miranda offered no answer.

"You can't send Kelly alone into Los Angeles in the middle of the night. She's never been away from here. She doesn't know anyone. She doesn't know your ... sister."

Miranda fidgeted.

"Wouldn't it be wiser to drive Kelly to Los Angeles? You and Eduardo could make sure she gets there safely and—"

Miranda's face screwed into a churlish scowl. "I want her gone! And there is no reason Eduardo needs to know where she is."

Elect Sun lifted her eyes and stared at Miranda with an unflinching gaze. Things she had not thought of saying in years, words she had exorcized when she discovered the true path to God, flooded her mind. She studied the woman before her and fought to control the tirade. Miranda was an exotic beauty that most men would find irresistible. How long did it take before they recognized who she really was?

Elect Sun saw Miranda look away nervously. She got an idea. Standing, she slowly removed her work gloves and stretched out her six-foot frame. She towered over Miranda.

"Here is what you *will* do." Elect Sun spoke as if to an unruly child. "You will travel with Kelly to Los Angeles yourself."

"I don't have the money to—"

Elect Sun silenced Miranda with a wave of her hand. "I will purchase the ticket for you. You will make sure I have the phone number of where Kelly can be reached, and you will have her contact me upon her arrival at your … *sister's*." The last word came out more harshly than Elect Sun intended.

Miranda stood speechless, like a child being punished. Elect Sun momentarily suffered the sin of pride for reading the woman correctly.

"Why should I?" Miranda pouted. "You have no right—"

"I will go to the police, Mrs. Garcia. I will tell them that you knew what was happening to your little girl. That you allowed her stepfather to have sex with her. That is a crime. Kelly's a minor. You are responsible for her by law. Do you want to go to prison?"

The woman's eyes widened. Elect Sun enjoyed the look of fear on Miranda's face, but the feeling was paired with guilt.

Miranda turned on her heel and stomped off.

After Miranda's car disappeared in a cloud of dust, Elect Peter found Elect Sun on her knees in the dirt, palms pressed together, head down, praying. He approached quietly and waited until she was once again trying to tame the weeds. Then he dropped to his knees and began working the ground with her.

"Do you want to talk?" He kept his eyes on the desiccated plants in the row before him.

Elect Sun brushed away some stray strands of gray hair with one hand. She told him about her conversation with Miranda and showed him the ticket for the Sunset Limited.

"I don't know how else you could have handled it," Elect Peter said. "Though I'm suddenly feeling a bit guilty. I would have enjoyed seeing Miranda cowed." A conspiratorial smile lit his face.

"It bothers me that I can still have bad feelings toward people," Elect Sun confessed.

"You know as well as I do that we are only human beings. We try to live the way Jesus taught us, but we all make mistakes. Some are not so horribly grievous." He smiled again, trying to lighten her mood, but consternation still etched Elect Sun's wrinkled face. "There is something else bothering you?"

Elect Sun sighed. "I should take Kelly to Los Angeles myself."

Elect Peter understood. "We have been here a long time. You would be of little help to the child in a city. Things have changed in the world since we came to this place. We should trust in the Lord. He will protect her."

"Sometimes the Lord wants us to help ourselves, Peter."

The old man thought for a moment. "Maybe we should ask Jason for his opinion. He's been out in the world. Maybe he can help."

15

THE BELL SOUNDED as the screen door to the Butterfield General Store opened and snapped closed. Tom Pace, never removing his eyes from the box scores, reached under the counter and grabbed a cardboard container that once held a shipment of Poore Brothers Potato Chips, Barbeque Style. When he looked up, he saw a haggard Jason Ramm standing before the counter.

"You don't look so good. You feelin' all right?" Tom shifted his reading glasses to the top of his head.

"Just tired." Ramm grabbed the box and moved down the aisle. Kelly needed protein, so he pulled three cans of Bumble Bee Tuna and three cans of sardines off the shelf. His hand hung in the air as he reached for a jar of Extra Crunchy Skippy Peanut Butter. He clenched his fingers into a tight fist to stop the shaking, then realized Tom was craning his neck, watching him. Their eyes met and the storekeeper returned to his paper.

Ramm took a deep breath. He had to relax. "Hey, Tom!" he said with false gaiety. "You got that feed yet?"

"Sure do," the store owner answered. He dropped the newspaper to the counter and stepped down from his stool.

"Got some forty-pounders of dog food back there, too, if you need it. Guess you're gonna be keepin' that dog?"

Ramm allowed himself a small smile. If Tom didn't get some piece of information from each of his customers every time they came in, he felt somehow unfulfilled. The dog was a good neutral subject. "Yes, I'll be keeping her. She's a nice dog. She has collar marks. Must have gotten lost."

"Or dumped," Tom said as he moved toward the store-room. "So many of them city people just drop 'em out here, thinkin' little Spotty can fend for hisself. Shit! It's better just puttin' a bullet in their heads."

The bell on the door jingled, but Ramm couldn't see anyone when he peered over the shelf. He heard the rustle of cellophane. He placed the box on the floor and walked up the aisle and around the corner. Kelly, head down, examined the wrapper on a package of chocolate chip cookies.

"Hello, Kelly."

Startled, she dropped the cookies and turned away from the voice. When she realized the man was not a stranger, she lifted her chin, and faced him. "Hi, Jason." She touched one hand to her bulging belly and rubbed it. "The baby's moving. Sometimes it kicks really hard. It doesn't hurt. Just feels a little strange."

"Put two bags a feed in your truck and a forty-pounder a dry dog food," Tom said, as he reentered the store. "Oh, hello, Kelly. Didn't realize you were here."

Kelly stared at her bare toes, while fishing a piece of paper from the pocket of her blue sundress. She handed the list to the shopkeeper.

"Let's see what we've got." Tom slipped reading glasses down from his forehead and eyed the neat script. "Okay.

Yep. Got it all. I'll have everything for you in just a minute."
He moved around the store collecting the items indicated
on the list. "Somebody goin' on a trip?"

"Yes, I am." Kelly bent over slowly in an effort to pick up
the cookies she'd dropped.

"I'll get that." Ramm walked over, retrieved the package,
and placed the cookies on the counter. She smelled of bath
soap.

"Getting ready for the hospital?" Tom pried. Kelly
shook her head. "No, I'm going away."

"Where?" Ramm asked.

"I'm going to stay with my aunt in Los Angeles."

"Who?" Tom placed toothpaste and shampoo on the
counter.

"My mother's sister, Lilliana."

Tom opened his mouth to speak, but just grunted
instead. He deposited her purchases in a plastic bag, then
picked up the cookies. "These, too? Don't see them on the
list."

"Oh, no. I don't have enough." Kelly shook her head.

"Put the cookies in the bag, Tom. I'll pay for them."

Kelly thanked Ramm, placed her money on the counter,
took the bag, and turned to leave. "Goodbye."

"Mother's sister, my ass!" Tom exclaimed when the
screen door snapped shut ringing the brass bell. "Miranda
ain't got no sister. No brother neither."

"Why would the woman lie?"

Tom looked up smiling, happy to divulge some of the
information he regularly collected. "My guess is Miranda's
jealous of the girl."

"Jealous? Of Kelly?"

"Who do you think made that baby?" Tom didn't wait for an answer. "Kelly's stepfather's took a likin' to her, and Miranda ain't never played second fiddle to nobody. She's one pissed off momma."

16

ELECT SUN HEARD the approaching vehicle and went outside to wait on the steps as the truck ground to a stop on the gravel drive.

"Are you all right, Kelly?" Ramm helped the girl from the vehicle.

"I'm fine. Just a little tired, but Jason and Dog gave me a ride from the store." Kelly handed the plastic bag containing the groceries to Elect Sun.

"Hurry inside now. Go upstairs and get washed. It's almost time for supper." Elect Sun turned and appraised Ramm as Kelly disappeared behind the screen door.

"You're not sleeping, Jason. Is there something wrong?"

Ramm took a deep breath, forced a smile. "I'm just sorting some things out." He followed Elect Sun into the shade of a sprawling cottonwood tree. Together they sat on the red cedar swing suspended from a broad, low-hanging branch.

"I need your advice." Elect Sun glanced up at the girl's corner room. "Miranda is insisting the child leave here."

"Kelly told me."

"I don't know what to do, Jason. Supposedly, Kelly's going to stay with Miranda's sister in Los Angeles, but ..."

"Miranda doesn't have a sister."

"How do you know?"

"Tom Pace."

"Of course. When in doubt, ask Tom."

"Where do you think Miranda is really sending her?"

Elect Sun paused. "I've been trying to figure that out. I insisted that she tell me where Kelly is going so we can stay in touch with her, but I'm not holding my breath. Miranda's biggest concern seems to be making sure Eduardo has no idea where Kelly is."

Their eyes met.

"Eduardo fathered the child," Elect Sun said.

Ramm nodded.

"Let me guess. Tom."

Ramm's lips lifted in a half smile. "Of course."

A breeze rippled through the leaves above, filling the air with white noise like the rushing of a shallow stream over smooth river rock. A pair of doves swooped down, gliding to a gentle stop in the grass at the base of the tree.

"Isn't there something we can do to help her? If only we could keep track of her. But in a city like Los Angeles, she'll be swallowed up. Lost."

Ramm had never seen Elect Sun look so defeated. Suddenly, he understood. "It's not your fault. I know how you feel about cities. Without the peace that surrounds you here you might get lost yourself."

Elect Sun gazed at the two gray birds, following them as they took off cooing into the cloudless desert sky. "I've lived in the city, Jason. Remember, I wasn't born in the desert. Why I have this fear, I don't know. Perhaps I'm afraid I won't be here when the time comes. I must be

81

ready for the end of God's clock. I've been waiting over thirty years."

Ramm considered the problem. "Here's what we'll do. I know some people in Los Angeles. People I've worked with." *People who get paid to track anyone I want them to.* "I'll make a few calls. We'll find out where Kelly is and keep an eye on her. You don't need to worry about a thing."

"Really?"

"Really."

"Good," Elect Sun smiled for the first time all day. "Then we must think about getting her back here. Her and the baby."

"One thing at a time," Ramm said. "Now, do you have any reason to believe Kelly's mother would physically harm her?"

"I know she has used physical force with the girl, but I can't say Kelly's been abused, except by Eduardo, of course." Elect Sun was quiet for a moment. "But that's a different kind of abuse. Miranda is self-centered and has certainly neglected Kelly …"

"And her ego has taken a big hit, but is she capable of anything worse than pettiness and neglect?"

"I don't know. I think she's just an overgrown, spoiled child who'll do nothing more than stamp her feet and pout in the hope of getting her way."

Ramm looked through the cottonwood branches toward the black basalt mountain that rose east of the compound. A thought occurred to him. "How does Miranda feel about money?"

"I have to assume she's never had much."

"Perhaps, we could make her an offer."

Elect Sun looked shocked. "You mean buy the child?"

"Sounds a little sick when you put it that way, but yes. That's what I mean."

The chains that held the swing tethered to the tree branch creaked as the seat moved back and forth. Dog, who'd been rooting around the yard, plopped down on the grass, flipped over, and stuck all four paws into the air, lying flat on her back. She wriggled around, apparently trying to scratch an itch.

"Oh, my!" Elect Sun gasped, her attention diverted when she saw the angry red marks, the swastika still clearly visible on the dog's belly.

Ramm patted her hand. "Don't worry about Dog. Or Kelly. We'll get this straightened out."

"But we don't have much money, Jason. Just a little saved up for emergencies."

"We'll work it out."

17

LATER THAT NIGHT, Ramm thumbed his way through the worn, second-hand Bible. The leather-bound book was gilt-edged, the letters tiny, ornate. The answers were in the book. Why couldn't he find them?

He shut his eyes and pinched the bridge of his nose in an effort to keep the headache at a bearable level. A quote came to him, not from the Bible, but rather from Shakespeare's *All's Well That Ends Well*.

"Our remedies oft in ourselves do lie, which we ascribe to heaven."

Ramm closed the book. Perhaps the answers were in him. He stood, intending to place the Bible back on the mantel, when he noticed a card sticking out of the pages. He slumped back into the corner of the couch and reopened the book, finding what he knew to be a Catholic memorial card placed on a page that read:

Ecclesiastes 5, The Value of a Friend.

Two are better than one, because they have a good reward for their labor. For if they fall, one will lift up his companion. But woe to him who is alone when he falls, for he has no one to help him up.

Ramm stared at the page. When was the last time he truly had a friend? His eyes burned with visions of a grinning soldier with white-blond hair, a boy whose long-ago death kept him forever young and strong, no memory able to age him. Then the fire.

"No!" Ramm rose and forced that nightmare away. He placed the card back into the Bible and noticed the date on the card was August 6, 1969. The memorial service for Robert T. Massi had been held at St. Jude's Catholic Church in Prescott, Arizona. St. Jude. The patron saint of lost causes. Perhaps the card was a sign he should convert. Perhaps the Roman Catholics could help him.

Ramm, amused at the thought, turned the card over. He froze, eyes riveted to the picture. Before him was the Virgin Mary with her sad blue eyes, arms outstretched beside her, palms up beckoning. She was draped in an azure gown, the folds falling gracefully to her feet where little children turned smiling faces upward to greet her. Though the countenance of Jesus's mother was a source of inspiration for artists for hundreds of years, he had not spent much time considering her face. Somehow, this one woman, whose actual features were unknowable, always seemed to look the same, regardless of the racial qualities ascribed to her. Whether Arab or Indian, African, Latina, or Asian, or even the ridiculous paintings that depicted the Semitic woman with blonde hair and blue eyes, like the one he held in his hands, the face and the expression always seemed the same. Her ever-present broken heart made portraying Mary as anything but a woman in despair—as any mother who had ever lost a child would be—impossible.

But Mary should have been joyous at the resurrection, her prayers answered along with all the other believers. Yet, in all of the museums and churches and galleries he'd visited, Ramm had not once seen the woman portrayed as anything but somber or grieving. There appeared not to be even a glint of happiness in the woman who bore Jesus.

He held the picture to the light, searching the face again, analyzing the melancholy countenance. Mary always appeared heartsick, devastated by the thought of what might have been.

He thought of the woman in Jerusalem.

The first time Ramm saw her, she was climbing the stairs to the Room of Pity inside the Church of the Holy Sepulcher. He had abandoned his surveillance of the target, while the old Hasid lunched with a friend at a noisy, outdoor cafe. With several hours to kill, his curiosity led him to the holy place said to be the exact location of the crucifixion.

He watched the woman move past the intricate glass mosaics as if in a trance, then into the darkened room. She paused briefly before the glittering altar at Golgotha and, without warning, dropped to her knees, face twisted in agony, and began crying out, desperate sobs reverberating off the ancient stones.

Ramm was transfixed by the spectacle. And that was when it had started.

18

BILLY CHECKED THE GLOWING dial on the watch with the camouflage band, yet another gift from Buck. He had about ten minutes, if the freight train was on time. Judging from the schedule, the Amtrak Sunset Limited should pass this section of track at about 1:10 a.m. Monday morning. He stepped across a three-foot joint, limping from the gash the dog bite had opened in his calf. He was able to ignore most of the pain, thanks to some self-medication in the form of a mixture of pot and Jack Daniel's. He counted as he went. Twenty-nine spikes and four bolts secured the track. The wiring, he knew, was pretty basic, and he'd have plenty of time, since there was little traffic on the antiquated line.

Billy saw the faint light in the distance and felt a surge of excitement. He'd read and reread the *SP Trainline* article, and picked the perfect location: on a trestle, near a curve that would encourage the train to tilt. Facing the oncoming train, he straddled the track, and watched as the locomotive approached. He'd seen a boy crushed by a train once—a game of "chicken" that the train had won in spectacular fashion. The boy's death had been quick, albeit messy, and hood lore had him down as a brave hero, as opposed to the drunken idiot Billy knew him to be. Still, you had to admire the guy for going out in style, a blaze of glory that left him splattered over three hundred yards of track. A death like that certainly beat wasting away on crack or shriveling up with AIDS.

Billy flung his arms wide and screamed into the desert wind. The train was less than a mile away. He saw only the light as it grew, a piercing beam that completely obscured the engine and the cars it pulled. The track rumbled beneath his feet.

Still, he waited.

"Five! Four! Three! Two! One!" Billy jumped, flailing his arms as he fell. He landed with a thud and a roll in the sandy wash below the track. The impact ripped open the dog bite, sending a bright stream of blood streaking down his leg. But Billy didn't care. He threw back his head and howled as the train roared above him.

"What's that for?" Ray asked, when he found Billy sitting before an ancient black Smith-Corona typewriter late the next morning.

"Typin' a letter from my grandpa. Least I can do."

"But your grandpa's dead, Billy." Ray scrunched up his face as if he were trying to figure out a tough math problem. "He can't write no letter."

"No shit, Ray. But Grandpa was always writin' letters. Pissed off about one thing or another. It was kind of his hobby. Look here." Billy tossed a bundle of envelopes held together with a thick red rubber band toward Ray. "Anytime somethin' happened Grandpa didn't like, he'd pull out this old typewriter, sit down, and write a letter. He was proud of 'em. Made these copies so he could read the letters to anyone who'd listen. Said that's why America was great. Anybody could say anything he wanted anytime."

"I guess your grandpa had a lot of complaints." Ray sat cross-legged on the ground and flipped through the pile of envelopes.

Billy nodded in agreement. "Especially after he got fired from the railroad. Grandpa said America was goin' down the toilet. All the niggers and spics and women's libbers fucked it all up. White guys just couldn't get a break any more." Billy eyed Ray. "Give me those!" Billy snatched the papers from the other boy's hands. "It's not like you're gonna read them or anything. Shit! Didn't you go to friggin' school?"

Ray frowned and looked away.

"Get me a beer!" Billy watched Ray shuffle toward the cooler. Something would have to be done about the boy. He couldn't leave him here to blab.

Billy pulled the sheet of paper from the typewriter. He was proud of the one-page diatribe dedicated to his grandfather, the only person on earth who he believed had ever given a good goddamn about him. The entire piece was composed of excerpts from the letters his grandfather had written. He titled it "Indictment of the ATF and the FBI," stealing the wording from letters addressed to the two government agencies the old man seemed to like the least. The opening narrative spoke of the government's bungling of the 1993 siege at Waco—the burning of David Koresh and his followers—and the shootings at Ruby Ridge.

Billy also picked out some obscure crimes with which his grandfather had been especially annoyed, one of which involved the shooting of a police officer's wife who knew too much about drug kickbacks.

He read the letter over, happy with the contents. But how should he sign it? His grandfather had always indorsed his letters with a large, bold signature, but, since he was dead, Carl James's name wouldn't work now, and Billy wasn't dumb enough to leave a trail that might lead back to him.

Still, he wanted to take the credit for the crime, wanted his homeboys to know he was the mastermind. Billy looked at the swastika etched into his arm, and remembered the pain from the razor and the black ink oozing from the broken Bic. His friends had referred to themselves as members of the Gestapo, claiming all blacks and Jews and Hispanics—anyone who wasn't one hundred percent Caucasian—as their targets. Needless to say, Billy had not ever mentioned his mother's heritage to anyone in that group.

Billy signed the letter "Sons of Gestapo". He read the page again and smiled.

He couldn't wait for the carnage to begin.

19

AS RAMM DROVE, a trail of iridescent dust swirled in the dusky light behind his pickup. On the front seat rested a coiled belt of supple brown calfskin into which a zipper had been sewn. He'd used the pouch countless times over the years to carry various forms of currency and the alternate identification papers that often became necessary in the course of his work. More than once, the extra cash and varied passports had saved his life.

As he passed the cemetery, he thought of Kelly and how she would sit placidly by her father's grave, a bouquet of flowers in her lap, the sad, unchangeable expression on her face. He touched his foot to the brake as a large dust devil surprised him, skipping over the low, rocky wall at the edge of the cemetery, whirling among the headstones, and spinning detritus high into the air. He eased the truck to a stop on the side of the road as a steady south wind blew in from the vast plain that stretched into the distance.

Ramm stepped out of the truck, transfixed by the dancing funnel as dried flowers rose from the graves of the long dead children. The bougainvillea branches were rendered into hundreds of individual petals, whirling specs of vermilion dotting the devil's vortex, which danced toward Ramm, then backed away, as if contemplating where it wished to go. At least three stories high, the dust devil steadied before him, launching small stones into the side of the truck, each one pinging off the metal frame. Grit stung his eyes. Then the funnel moved and cooler air encircled him; red petals swirled in a dizzying dance. He raised his palms and was suffused with a sense of calm, a promise of peace.

In a matter of seconds, the dust devil moved away, and the early evening desert heat enveloped him once again. Stunned, Ramm watched the sandy shaft move over the desert. The funnel drew him. Irrationally, he wanted to follow.

Later that evening, the dining table in the compound was set for supper.

"Please sit, everyone." Elect Sun placed a large bowl of spaghetti next to a white pitcher filled with steaming tomato sauce, heavy with garlic and a hint of fresh basil.

The Children of Light moved to their seats, their attention diverted as Elect Peter made his way down the stairway. He carried a small, battered suitcase. Kelly walked slowly behind him, her hand clutching the railing as she descended.

Ramm entered silently and placed the leather pouch on the massive oak sideboard that stretched the length of the room. He noted Elect Sun's solicitous look and, when he realized the concern was for him, felt a sudden urge to bolt.

"Take that seat, Jason." Elect Sun indicated the one at the head of the capacious table.

The Children were somber as they ate. Kelly had added a dimension to their lives they had long been without. They enjoyed having the young girl around and had looked forward to the arrival of the baby.

The girl, who had not spoken during the meal, kept her head down and didn't respond.

Elect Sun looked pleadingly at Ramm.

Ramm wiped his mouth with a cloth napkin. "Um … yes, Kelly. I'm certain you'll be surprised by the things you'll see in Los Angeles."

Elect Sun nodded in agreement.

"There are parks. And the zoo. I bet you've never seen an elephant. Or a zebra."

Kelly turned toward Ramm. "No, I've seen pictures, in books. What other animals do they have at this zoo?"

"I remember a trip to the zoo." Elect Sarah's face lit up at the memory. "I was just a little girl, but I will never forget …"

During the remainder of the meal, the Children of Light recounted for Kelly all the zoo and animal tales from their varied pasts. There was laughter in the house, and though this was a temporary solution to their sadness, Elect Sun was grateful for the reprieve. She was adamant that this night, which might be Kelly's last at the compound, should be a happy memory for the child.

With the dinner dishes done and Kelly in bed for a nap, Elect Sun and Elect Peter sat in the swing beneath the cottonwood's dark canopy. Ramm leaned against the great trunk, rubbing the soft calfskin pouch between his fingers.

"These friends of yours, are you sure they'll keep track of her?" Elect Peter stared at Ramm.

"Absolutely." He'd made sure the men would watch and protect Kelly well by offering them twice their normal fee, imparting that, should anything happen to the girl or her baby, he would deal with the watchers personally. "She'll be all right, until we can get something else worked out. And she'll have cash." He held up the pouch.

Elect Sun shook her head. "Kelly's never dealt with money, except for her trips to the General Store. She doesn't know anything about fiscal responsibility."

"Don't worry. I'll speak with her. I'll explain that the money is only for emergencies."

Elect Peter edged his wiry frame off the swing. "I think I'll go put together a small medical kit for Kelly. Band-Aids, ointment, that kind of thing."

When Elect Peter had gone, Ramm sat next to Elect Sun, causing the old swing to creak under his weight.

"I think he's just trying to keep busy." She nodded in the doctor's direction. She turned to Ramm, laying her weathered hand on his arm. "You're losing weight, Jason. I'm worried about you."

He turned away, unable to look at her, lest she see his lie. He stared up through the cottonwood branches into the clear night sky.

"Jason, I hope you know you can come to me with whatever is bothering you. Perhaps, I can help. Or maybe you'd rather speak with Elect Peter, if it is something you don't wish to discuss with a woman."

Ramm furtively rubbed away the tear that escaped down his cheek.

"I'll go fix you some chamomile tea," Elect Sun said, patting his arm.

Kelly watched from her bedroom window as Elect Sun crossed the lawn. Jason remained motionless in the old wooden swing.

She couldn't sleep. Why was she being sent away? Why couldn't she stay here with the Children? Why had she never heard her mother speak of Aunt Lilliana?

Kelly spent her final hours with the Children listening to the yips of distant coyotes and gazing out the second-story window at stars that glittered across the vast desert sky like a spill from a voluminous sugar bowl.

20

RAMM DROVE THE TWO MILES to the Hyder Station. Gravel crunched beneath the truck's tires, air whooshed through the open windows. There had been no rain in weeks, so the desert smelled of dust with a hint of pungent creosote.

Kelly sat in the middle. Elect Sun held her hand tightly in an effort to calm the girl. In a matter of minutes, they were parked next to the concrete slab that was the station. A sign suspended from an aluminum pole simply said *Hyder*—the word positioned above the Southern Pacific Railroad logo.

Ramm spotted Miranda. Dressed in a bright red, spaghetti-strap shirt, tight black jeans, and black cowboy boots, she was hard to miss. A cigarette dangled from full crimson lips. She was alone. Eduardo Garcia had not come to say goodbye.

Ramm carried the suitcase, while Kelly clung to Elect Sun's hand. As they approached Miranda, the girl's gait slowed.

"Mrs. Garcia," Elect Sun nodded curtly when they stepped onto the concrete.

Miranda blew a thick stream of smoke into the air between them, but said nothing. Then she turned her dark, almond-shaped eyes to Ramm. The edges of her painted lips—a color that matched her shirt—turned up in a coy smile.

"I don't believe we've met," she cooed. "Surely you are not a member of the Children of Light. I mean, that would be such a waste, now wouldn't it?"

"Jason Ramm." He set the suitcase on the concrete and extended his hand. "Elect Sun and I are old friends," he added with an abundance of disingenuous charm.

"Why Sun, you surprise me." Miranda purred. "Hiding this strapping man all for yourself."

Elect Sun, shocked by the exchange, didn't respond. The train's whistle sounded, and the engine's headlight appeared down the track. Elect Sun turned to Kelly and busied herself straightening the collar on the girl's cotton dress. "Now you must remember to wear your shoes. One can't go traipsing around a city barefoot."

Miranda continued to boldly appraise Ramm. She made no attempt to talk to Kelly.

"Don't you have a sweater or a coat?" Ramm asked the girl. "It might get cold on the train. And Los Angeles is not like the desert."

Kelly shook her head.

"Just a minute." Ramm loped back to the truck and fished a huge dark blue U.S. Navy sweatshirt out of the back of the cab.

"I've only worn it a couple of times," he said when he returned. "It's kind of big, but I think it'll come in handy."

"Thank you." Kelly cradled the sweatshirt in her arms.

Her face remained, as always, expressionless. Still, Ramm was learning to detect subtle changes in the girl's eyes. He could tell she was pleased.

The engineer at the helm of the Sunset Limited forced the train to a halt with a steel-on-steel screech. Elect Sun bent, kissing Kelly on the cheek as the train's doors snapped open.

"You have the tickets?" Miranda pitched the cigarette to the ground, grinding the butt with a twist of her boot.

Ramm removed a package from the inside pocket of his jacket.

Miranda reached over, took the envelope, and made an obvious show of running her fingers down the back of his hand. Then Ramm beamed a grin at Miranda and the woman flashed a dazzling smile of her own. Kelly's mother, never looking at the child, picked up her own bag and sauntered toward the train.

Elect Sun frowned.

Ramm turned to Kelly. "Remember what I told you." He patted her right hip, keeping his voice low so Miranda wouldn't hear.

"I won't tell anyone."

"No one at all," he reminded her. He'd explained earlier that even Miranda should not know about the money she was carrying.

The girl nodded. "I understand."

Ramm lifted her chin. "You have no reason to be afraid of anything. We've made sure of that. And before you know it, you and the baby will be back here with the Children. Okay?"

Kelly took a deep breath. She picked up her suitcase. "Okay," she whispered.

Elect Sun and Ramm stood silently as they watched the girl disappear onto the train. Their eyes met, a question hanging between them.

"Give me a little more credit than that," Ramm said as they walked back toward the truck.

"Well, it was pretty obvious that—"

"I certainly hope Miranda thought so." He smiled.

Elect Sun cocked her head.

Ramm put his arm around the woman's shoulders as they walked. "Flies and honey, Elect Sun. Flies and honey."

$$\psi$$

On the train, mother and daughter sat separated by an empty seat. Miranda on the aisle, Kelly by the window. With her mother already engrossed in a magazine, Kelly turned and was surprised by her own reflection in the dark glass. She rarely looked at herself in the mirror. Kelly turned her face slowly one way, then the other, and tried to establish the exact reason people reacted to her the way they did. Other than Miranda and the female members of the Children of Light, she had never had much contact with other women, and she didn't watch much television— the reception was bad and they had no cable or satellite dish. She had never been to a movie. The only hints Kelly had about what she was supposed to look like were gleaned from the fashion magazines Miranda was constantly leafing through.

She studied her ink-black hair and blue eyes, so unlike her mother's, the one link she had to Bryan Kelly's Irish ancestors. Her ears were small, lips full, skin tawny and clear, perhaps a shade or two lighter than Miranda's. She remembered the way her mother smiled at Ramm, lips pulled up presenting two rows of perfect white teeth. She'd seen him smile back. Kelly glanced at Miranda, then turned to face the window again. She tried to smile.

Tried again.

And again.

But the face in the window remained lifeless, a quiescent mask. Kelly finally gave up and glanced at her mother's stony profile. Was Miranda ignoring her because she was angry about the baby or because she was embarrassed to be sitting with her in front of strangers on the train?

A man wearing a red cap, white shirt, and gray pants with a navy-blue stripe down the side approached them.

"Tickets please." He smiled.

Kelly was tempted to turn away, but forced herself to look straight at the man. If her face startled him, he failed to show it. He took a portion of each ticket, handed the remainder back to Miranda, then thanked them, and moved down the aisle.

By the time the Sunset Limited pulled out of the station, Ramm had deposited Elect Sun on the steps of the compound, and was on his way back to the cabin. He passed the graveyard, headstones ghostly apparitions in the glare of the headlights. Turning left, he drove along the eastern edge of the basalt mountain where the dust devil had danced earlier in the day. Rows of long-dead palm trees—planted by someone with good intentions, but who, for some reason, left them to wither—rose like sentinels into the night sky. Ramm's head ached as he turned onto Hyder Road, which flanked the Southern Pacific Railroad tracks.

21

THOUGH BILLY HAD CHECKED and rechecked his work, he decided to go over the preparations one last time. The *SP Trainline* article, written as a historical perspective, outlined the procedure step-by-step. The Southern Pacific track—like the one in Harney, Nevada in 1939—consisted of old-fashion jointed rail, not the welded variety used on lines that carried high volumes of traffic. Billy had unbolted the steel plate that held two sections of the track together. He'd removed twenty-nine spikes and an eighteen-pound steel bar that connected the two, thirty-nine-foot sections. The article explained that the pressure of the wheels on the rail would force one section laterally outside the other, causing the wheels to go between them, derailing the train.

The next part had been a little trickier. By disconnecting the rails, Billy separated the bond wire that constantly carried a low power signal current that was used primarily to let the railroad companies know the exact location of their trains. But the bond wire also allowed crews to detect any trouble along the line on which they were traveling. The current, disrupted by his work, would signal the engineer that there had been a break in the line, making him stop the train prior to reaching the damaged rail. The problem was solved by running a wire between the rails, bypassing the broken cable, and disabling the electrical sensors, so the engineer would not receive the red-light warning indicating there was trouble ahead.

"Come on, Billy!" Ray glanced nervously down the track toward Hyder.

Finally satisfied that he'd prepared everything properly, Billy folded the *SP Trainline* magazine and placed the issue into the back waistband of his grimy jeans. "Shit! I almost forgot!" He hurried to the edge of the ravine where he picked up several copies of the letter. He smiled again at his Sons of Gestapo signature, then scattered the epistle strategically around the area. Billy didn't know where the train would land and he wanted to make sure the letter was found.

Ignoring Ray's pleas to get away, Billy stood for a moment staring up the track. He slipped a fat, neatly rolled joint out of his shirt pocket, and moistened the paper with his saliva. He struck a match, cupped the flame in his hand to shield the tiny blaze from the desert wind, and lit the end. Billy inhaled, filled his lungs, and listened to the pop of burning seeds. He held his breath, enjoyed the acrid smoke, then exhaled. After another toke, he checked the luminous green dial on his watch.

Then he saw a spark of light in the distance.

"Come on, Ray! Let's get up to where we can see the show." He pinched off the end of the joint and tucked the rest into his shirt pocket.

The boys hurried away, moving north over the rocky ground. Though Billy could normally outrun Ray easily, he still suffered from wounds inflicted by the dog and his tangle with the cholla, so he quickly fell behind. Still, both boys crested what was the nearest of several basalt mountains in plenty of time.

Most of the two hundred and forty-eight passengers on the Sunset Limited were asleep when David Flowers—weaving slightly as the sleeper car rattled along at fifty miles-per-hour—moved along the passageway en route to the bathroom. At the end of the car he saw Mitchell Bates, a twenty-year Amtrak veteran.

"Don't forget to wake me up when we get to Palm Springs," Flowers said. "Don't wanna sleep through my stop."

"Don't you worry about a thing." Bates grinned. "That's what they pay me for."

Two cars back, Kelly cupped her hands around her eyes and pressed tightly to the window. She could see the moonlit desert careening by, the scattered mountains black against a star-filled night sky. She let her body sway with the gentle rolling of the car, a strangely pleasant sensation, and thought about the sense of calm that surrounded her. Maybe it was because, for the first time since her father died, there were other people who cared about her. Kelly glanced over at Miranda, still engrossed in a two-month-old, dog-eared issue of *Glamour Magazine*. Had her mother ever had a friend?

Up in the cab, the engineer watched as the massive headlight bathed the track ahead in bright white light. He'd been on this run hundreds of times. Just ahead, was a curve that would lead the train onto a trestle that spanned one of the deeper washes between Phoenix and Los Angeles. The headlight blazed—a star shooting in the darkness—wrapping the track in light as harsh as any clear desert day.

But the damage was under the rails where no light could penetrate.

Ramm gripped the steering wheel as he headed back to his cabin. That edgy, too-much-caffeine feeling had taken hold again. Guilt assaulted him. He should be on the train protecting Kelly. And had he made a mistake in contacting the watchers? Had the move put him in play again? The community in which he'd worked for so many years was relatively small, and there was always the possibility that word had spread about the debacle in Jerusalem. By contacting the watchers, he might have put himself in jeopardy, which could also bring harm to those around him.

Ramm's head pounded, the incipient migraine accompanied by a hazy aura. He knew his psychological state was fluctuating. How long could he stay ahead of the problem without medication? What if he blacked out again? What if he was hospitalized and people started checking on his background? Frustrated and powerless, he cursed and jammed on the breaks. The truck skidded to a stop on the soft shoulder where blacktop and dirt merged at the turnoff. He rubbed his face hard, then he looked up and peered through the windshield. Ramm blinked several times, confused.

There, in the night sky before him, floating in a spectral light, was Kelly's face. Ramm squinted, shut his eyes tight, then looked again. The ghostly image was still there, hovering before him, her troubled visage beckoning him to follow. She merged with paintings and sculptures—the mother of Jesus in all her quiet grief, the face of Mary on the shimmering white marble of Michelangelo's St. Peter's Pieta, on Raphael's Madonna del Granduca, her desolate melancholy depicted by Masaccio, Veneziano, and countless other artists through time.

Ramm painfully unclenched his hands from around the steering wheel and blinked into the darkness. Then Kelly's face disappeared, replaced by a bright light that splashed over the desert. The suddenness of the brilliant beam's appearance caught him off guard. He tried to focus, then grabbed for the loaded Glock he kept under the front seat. But when the blazing light splashed past, followed by the steady beat of passing railcars, he relaxed.

Then, an unexpected wave of heat engulfed him, and he pushed open the cab door and stepped out, breathing deeply, trying to clear his head. The noise hit him like a blow, shattering the desert calm. Reflexively, Ramm dropped to the ground and listened to the calamitous groaning, a ghastly noise that washed over him like a rogue wave.

Kelly felt the train car rock hard to one side, then heard the screech of metal-on-metal. For a moment, she sensed a weightlessness and was lifted from her seat as if by an invisible hand. The passenger car tilted and fell sideways. Passengers, jolted awake, screamed as the desert floor roared up at them. Then, nothing but black.

22

THE CALL WENT OUT from the Sunset Limited immediately. The engineer, trained for emergencies, forced himself to remain under control as he radioed for help. In a matter of minutes, calls were relayed to Phoenix, Yuma, and Gila Bend for all emergency medical units, and to local and state police and nearby military bases for help securing the area. Within fifteen minutes, an army of police and medical personnel were en route, followed closely by a mass of reporters whose radio, television, and newspaper outlets had a policy of continually monitoring police scanners.

Up on the mountain, Billy howled. The engine had managed to cross the trestle, but eight cars behind it derailed. He watched rapt in almost orgasmic gratification. A baggage car, a dormitory car, two sleepers, a diner, a lounge car, and two coaches had jumped off the track, four plunging into the wash thirty feet below.

Billy picked up the binoculars. As he watched, screams rose from the wreck site, first just a few, but in a matter of minutes, the voices became a chorus of pain and fear. He could see someone crawling in the sand, and another man who staggered, a bone sticking out of his pants at a perverse angle. Billy scanned the area and focused on the engine. The light shone inside the car, and he could see the engineer on the phone, surprisingly calm. He refocused on the train cars in the wash where passengers and crew were now appearing from the wreckage. Some clutched their bloodied bodies and wandered aimlessly in shock. Others helped the seriously injured.

"It's fucking great, isn't it, Ray? Here. Take a look." Keeping his eyes on the carnage below, Billy extended the binoculars toward Ray.

"No, thanks." Ray turned away.

Billy glared at the boy, who was flat on his back, fat tears rolling down his cheeks.

"What the fuck's the matter with you?" Billy hurled the binoculars, hitting Ray in the stomach, causing him to curl into a fetal position. The boy was sobbing.

"You're missing a kick-ass show, Ray!" Billy crawled like an insect, retrieved the binoculars, and focused again on the twisted train and broken people emerging from within.

Then, he saw something else. Just beyond the wreckage, south of the wash, headlights stood fixed in the darkness.

$$\psi$$

Jason Ramm was on his knees, immobilized by the destruction before him. Victims struggled out of the broken cars, frantic, bloodied. Some staggered, dazed. Still others screamed in fear at the sight of their own wounds or hysterically as they searched for loved ones. The chaos elicited old memories, similar scenes of confusion and panic. He remembered a Napalmed village. Burning people trying desperately to scatter in the wake of the incendiary greeting cards. A woman, clutching a charred child—tiny body smoking, features blotted by burns—holding the baby out to him as if he could transform the dead lump of flesh back into a living, breathing child.

"No! No! Not now!" Ramm beat his fists on the rocky ground, hoping the pain might prevent him from succumbing to the madness. He shook his head, tried to clear the burnt baby away. The woman and her dead infant were replaced by the twisted wreckage of the Sunset Limited.

He rose and sprinted across the narrow expanse of desert, calculating where Kelly might be. He scanned the wreck site as he ran, eliminated the baggage car and the sleepers. Ramm focused so intently on the girl's whereabouts, he didn't see the twisted roots. His foot caught, and he sprawled to the hard-packed desert floor. Ramm's right hand slammed into a jagged quartz boulder, slicing his palm, separating the flesh as cleanly as a surgeon's scalpel. He breathed heavily and stared at the wound. The free-flowing blood and the pain centered him.

Ramm raised himself slowly, then stood motionless. Forgetting the injury, he surveyed the scene below with cold detachment.

He ran again, but now his pace was measured, even. Entering the wash, he encountered the broken bodies of the injured, but ignored their anguished cries, and swept callously past them, obsessed with his quest to locate the girl. The first car he approached lay completely on its side. Two men struggled as they lifted an elderly, heavyset woman up through a door. Ramm hoisted himself onto a spot just below a row of blown-out windows and began systematically working his way down the outside of the car. He peered into the darkened interior at intervals of five feet. Dull emergency lights flickered, illuminating the injured and those administering aid.

Kelly was not among them. Ramm searched the second car and, again, did not find the girl. The third car hung precariously, rear wheels still touching the track while the front end perched atop another car that lay sideways in the wash. Ramm jumped up, grabbing the top of the car, ignoring the pain in his ripped right hand, and pulled himself onto the roof. But the pitch made holding on difficult. Flipping his legs around, he eased them over the side that faced up at a forty-five-degree angle. He felt for the lip of the window, but his foot touched solid glass. Ramm thrust his knee into the pane several times, but the window wouldn't give, so he edged his way down to the next one. The second window had blown out, allowing him a place to perch. He let go of the roof, grabbed the top side of the window frame, and slid inside the car.

Emergency lights sputtered on and off. A man, sixtyish and balding, blood running from a grotesquely broken nose, reached out for help. Ramm ignored him, crawled over the tilted seats, and methodically scanned each victim. He passed a woman in her mid-twenties, unconscious, with a compound fracture of the right leg. A teenage boy, arms wrapped tightly around his ribcage, mumbled in a foreign language Ramm recognized as Finnish.

"Sir, could you give me a hand here?" a middle-aged woman in a running suit asked. "I'm a nurse and this man …"

Ramm ignored her and moved down the aisle without a word.

He saw Miranda first. Even in the murky half-light her brilliant red shirt was hard to miss. Crumpled on her side, sprawled up against the bottom of the seats, bleeding from a head injury, she bore no resemblance to the *lamia* who had stroked the back of his hand less than half-an-hour earlier. Ramm scanned the area around Miranda, finding nothing. He continued on to the next seat, and the next, but Kelly wasn't there. Had she been out of her seat when the train derailed?

Then he saw her. The girl's small frame was bunched up behind her mother, hidden in the darkness by the dark blue sweatshirt. Hauling Miranda out of the way—showing no concern for any injuries she might have sustained—he cautiously examined Kelly. Her breathing was steady. He felt no obvious broken bones. A large contusion swelled on the left side of her head where she had probably been thrown into the window.

He lifted her in his arms, startled by the weight of her body. Moving steadily, but slowly over the seats, Ramm made his way to the end of the car, stepping over prostrate bodies and scattered luggage. At the door, he placed Kelly on the upturned side of a seat and lifted himself through the opening. Then, he leaned down through the doorway, and pulled her up by the arms.

A bulky teenager with short-cropped black hair and a goatee watched Ramm from below and came to help. Together, they eased Kelly off the front end of the dangling car, onto the side of the one below, and finally down into the uneven sand of the wash.

Ramm paused, brushed the hair out of Kelly's face, and recalled the sky vision.

"We better get someone to help her." The boy pointed at Kelly's bulging belly. "I heard a woman say she was a nurse and—"

Before the boy had a chance to finish, Ramm scooped her up, and sprinted off into the darkness. He'd gone about fifty yards when the single sheet of typed paper caused him to stop and look. Resting undamaged on the ground, away from the rest of the litter of the wreckage, the overly large, dark signature caught his attention. Ramm knelt to read it, still cradling the unconscious girl in his arms.

A few minutes later, breathing hard from the exertion of the run, Ramm set Kelly gently on the front seat of the truck and brushed the blue-black hair from her inanimate face. He froze, unable to look away. His heart rate slowed. He was engulfed by an overwhelming sense of calm. Tears tracked down his dusty cheeks. He couldn't take her back. *She* was the answer.

Ramm closed the door, then walked around the front of the pick-up, but he stopped, a prickling sensation crawling up his spine. Someone was watching. He strode deliberately to the driver side door and got in, then Ramm reached behind the seat for the binoculars and methodically scanned the area.

He found what he was looking for on one of the mountains rising above the chaos of the wreck site. The boy, with his own set of binoculars, was watching *him*. The kid with the swastika, the one who'd attacked Kelly and carved up Dog. Now the signature on the letter made sense. He struggled with the realization that the boy had seen him carry Kelly out of the wash, had watched him place the girl in the truck.

Ramm had a problem.

23

RAMM KICKED THE DOOR open, and moved swiftly through the cabin and into the bedroom. He placed Kelly on the bed, checking her a second time for injuries. The bruise above her left eye, swollen and red, appeared to be the only damage she'd sustained.

After covering her with a quilt, he pulled the worn oak rocker to the side of the bed and sat. Ramm considered his options. He should get Kelly to a doctor, but then they'd know where she was. They'd take her from him. Discomfited by the thought, Ramm worked the rocker hard, as he tried to figure out what to do. He ran a hand over the top of his scalp, then leaned forward, cupping his face in both hands, and placed his elbows on the edge of the bed. Where was the man who made only logical, calculated moves? He'd always been sharply decisive.

Kelly mumbled something, but did not wake. Ramm stared at the girl and studied her face. A quiet descended, calming him. His thoughts slowed. Clarity returned.

In a matter of minutes, he was dressed in gray and black camouflage. A black wool cap covered his head. Black face paint darkened all but his eyes, which reflected a ghostly blue. He strapped the eight-inch, bone-handled steel blade—one side smooth and lethally sharp, the other serrated with quarter-inch teeth—to his thigh. He laced on heavy, black, all-terrain boots, then pulled on thin black leather gloves that enveloped his hands like a second skin. He carried no identification.

Ramm walked to the bed and looked down at the sleeping girl. Her face was peaceful, her ink-colored hair strewn across the pillow. He checked her pulse, pressing two fingers against her slender wrist. The beat was strong and even. As he turned to go, Ramm caught his own reflection in the mirror above the dresser. The doppelganger staring back was who he really was. He would never escape that man. He felt a familiar thrill surge through him. Reaching down, he caressed the smooth bone handle of the knife, an old friend. Perhaps he really didn't want to change.

The dog whined, thumping her tail on the polished pine floor. "No, Dog. Stay!" he whispered, motioning to the animal to lie at the foot of the bed. Then Ramm eased the door closed silently behind him and slipped away.

The bit slid easily into the Appaloosa's mouth. He decided against the saddle, since he might have to set her loose. After leading the horse out of the corral, he grasped hold of her mane and hoisted himself onto the animal's back. Ramm kicked her sharply in the ribs, sending them both hurtling toward the ridge that would lead them back to the Sunset Limited.

Two passengers lifted a body out of the train, gently

laying the victim on the soft sand of the wash. An Amtrak employee came over to help.

"Mitch! Oh my God, Mitchell Bates." He removed his cap.

"Is that man dead?" a woman shrieked from nearby.

"Let's get a blanket and cover him," the Amtrak employee said. "Before people start freaking out."

ψ

"It's about fucking time." Billy watched the people below drape the inert body with a blanket. He scanned the wreck site again, looking for more fatalities, and was disappointed to see most of the victims moving about without aid. Billy hoped they were perhaps leaving the more mangled bodies on the train until help arrived. He was glad Ray seemed uninterested and didn't want to use the binoculars, as he could not tear himself away from the wonderfully tragic tableau he had created.

He watched as another victim was eased out of a sleeper car, and was disappointed when, upon scanning the body, he found no monstrously gaping wounds. The cat he'd disemboweled when he was thirteen came to mind. The pathetic creature had screeched hideously as it staggered around unraveling its own intestines. That's what Billy wanted to see. Something as cool as that. But victim after victim left him unfulfilled. Most of the injuries appeared to be minor.

The sound that distracted him was faint at first. Billy listened intently and soon recognized the *thwump thwump thwump* of helicopter rotors. He rolled over on his back, the dark night sky pushing him into the black basalt stones.

"Come on, Ray. We gotta leave." Billy preferred to stay and watch the show below, but he didn't want to get caught. He yanked Ray up by his collar and saw the boy was still crying. "You fucking pussy!" He spat the words in disgust. He would have to do something about Ray.

The blue Chevy, packed full with Buck's belongings, and a few empty beer cans scattered around the cold fire ring were all that remained of the boys' presence at the cave. Ramm checked the car doors. They were locked.

He heard the choppers. He would have to be quick. He slipped silently up the mountain and untied the horse. After knotting the reins on her neck, he slapped the Appaloosa on the rump and sent her galloping into the darkness.

Ramm crouched behind a basalt boulder, one that afforded an unimpeded view of the area in which he'd be working. He'd seen the boys bolt up the hill. He knew they'd be back soon.

AFTER

24

JACK COOPER'S CELLPHONE sounded. He rolled over and grabbed the phone from the bedside table, an original old Shaker piece he'd painstakingly refinished to remove water rings and cigarette burns left by idiots who didn't appreciate fine craftsmanship. The illuminated phone face informed him the time was one thirty-five a.m.

"Oh, please! Leave me alone, Buddy. I am not on call tonight."

"Coop!"

"Come on. I know I owe you for that little prank, but—"

"No joke, Coop. I need everyone. A train's derailed near Hyder."

"Shit! I'm sorry. When I saw the message, I just thought you were yankin' my chain."

"Yea, fine. Get your ass out there."

"Hold on. Let me get a pen." Cooper jotted down the location.

"How long 'til you can get there?" Buddy asked.

"About thirty minutes."

"Haul ass. They need help coordinating evacuation of the injured."

"Are there a lot of them?" Cooper yawned, and pulled on his pants, while cradling the phone between his shoulder and ear.

"They're saying it looks like a war zone out there."

"You mean it was a passenger train? Geez, Buddy. I was picturing a lot of dumped freight."

"It's Sunday night, dearie. Well, Monday morning actually."

"Oh my God! The Sunset Limited?"

"Yes, indeed."

"Shit!"

"And here's some more shit for you, my friend. You'll be taking charge of dealing with the media. The horde is no doubt preparing to descend, even as we speak."

"Gee, thanks."

Cooper, whose old adobe home stood on five wild desert acres ten miles west of Gila Bend, headed north on Painted Rock Damsite Road, passing the cultivated fields of Dendora Ranch, then the almost invisible track that led to the Rowley Mine site. He turned east just before the dam at the Gila River, then, after taking numerous unnamed switchbacks, found himself heading west paralleling the Southern Pacific Railroad tracks.

Cooper spotted the helicopters—some coming, some going—their lights cutting through the clear desert night. Despite the vast number of aircraft moving in and out, he was still stunned by the enormity of the devastation when he finally arrived at the wreck site. Almost a dozen other police vehicles were already on the scene.

As he jumped out of his four-wheel-drive Blazer, Cooper noticed far too few medical personnel had arrived. He knew many would be en route, but the site was remote, direct access limited. He and the other first responders performed triage, separating the seriously injured from the rest of the victims. He noted that many of the passengers were elderly and that relatively few appeared to be seriously hurt. The fact that many had been sleeping when the train derailed had protected them, to a certain extent. They hadn't seen the disaster coming, had not tensed at the moment of impact, much like a drunk driver is relaxed at the wheel, and so frequently walks away from an accident unharmed.

A line of ambulances appeared in the distance, a convoy with signal lights whirling, casting an eerie glow.

"Here's a man who can help you, miss." Cooper passed a frightened older teen over to the ministrations of a Yuma County paramedic.

"Let's check that arm," the medic said cheerfully, as he reached for the afflicted appendage the girl cradled tightly to her chest. He nodded at Cooper, indicating the deputy was free to move on.

25

THE BOYS, BREATHING IN GASPS, scrambled up
the dirt track and headed for the Chevy. Billy reached into
his pocket, grabbed the key, and unlocked the driver-side
door. Ray fidgeted, scanning the area as he waited for Billy
to let him in. Hopped up on the carnage he'd witnessed,
a sudden urge to kill seized Billy, a teasing sensation that
promised a kind of release.

The gun was hidden under the front seat, but the sound
of a shot might draw attention to them. Billy paused and
looked at Ray. He had a knife, but then what would he do
with the body? The car was packed with all the stuff he'd
stolen from Buck. There'd surely be blood all over the car if
he had to shove the little pussy inside. Billy finally decided
he'd have to take care of Ray later. He'd savor the thought,
a little something to look forward to.

The figure stepped silently out of the darkness and,
without a wasted motion, grabbed Ray, one arm strapped
across the boy's thin chest, the other hand holding tightly to
his head. With one smooth jerk, he snapped the boy's neck.

Horrified, Billy was unable to move. Ray's motionless
body slipped silently to the ground. Despite the face paint,

he knew the man. He willed his legs to move, but they remained frozen, as if in a nightmare when there is no escaping the monster. In an instant, the man was behind him. Billy glanced right, then left, looking for a way out.

The man waited patiently for Billy to make a move. The boy yanked open the car door, rusted hinges creaked. In an instant, a large, gloved hand closed tightly over Billy's mouth. The blade slipped from its black leather sheath. Billy fought and kicked, but he was no match for the professional whose hand wrapped around his face like cold steel. The big man held the knife before the boy, taunting. The blade glinted in the silvery desert moonlight.

Billy's eyes widened in horror.

Helicopters appeared from behind the mountains, their rotors singing in staccato rhythm. Noise didn't matter now. The man shifted the boy, sinking his knee into Billy's spine. He wrapped one arm across the boy's chest and laid the flat edge of the chilled metal blade against Billy's throat.

The boy screamed.

Starting just below the left ear at the edge of the jaw, the man made a deep slice into Billy's jugular, and then slowly dragged the blade across the dying boy's throat.

ψ

With helicopters moving in fast, Ramm had no time to waste. He was banking on the probability that the police teams would be concentrating their efforts on the wreck below. He wiped the knife clean on the shoulder of Billy's shirt, sheathed the blade and, careful not to get any blood on himself, lifted the tail of the boy's flannel shirt, wrapping the material tightly around the gaping neck wound. Ramm opened the car door, hoisted the body into the middle of the front seat, and reached over to unlock the passenger-side door. Then he stepped around the car to Ray's prostrate form. Luckily, Ray was small, so he was able to stuff the boy into the front seat along with Billy.

The helicopters were flying in low now, their mechanical hum like the song of giant insects. Ramm cringed as the ubiquitous Vietnam music played around him, sound that had mutated into a field vet's lullaby, a chorus he knew to be the ultimate white noise. He thought of Kelly, shook his head, composed himself, and concentrated on the task at hand.

The keys. The boy had been holding them. Ramm checked the body and found nothing. He looked under the seat, in the ignition, then, outside the car on the ground. He found the keys dropped by the left front tire.

Ramm wasted no motion moving to the fire ring. He gathered up empty cans and every tiny scrap of paper that might show someone had recently camped in the spot. Breaking a bushy branch from the far side of a mesquite tree—a clean snap at a spot inside and high on the trunk facing away from the campsite—he swished the leaves gently across the ground inside the shallow cave and the area outside by the fire ring, erasing any evidence of human occupation. He backed his way to the car, wiping out his own boot prints as he went. Standing on the inside of the doorframe, he scanned the area one last time. Then he tossed the branch over the side of the mountain.

Ramm drove slowly, not wanting to draw attention to the blue Chevy, and turned away from the site of the wreckage when the road veered northwest. The car was leaving tracks in the dry dirt, but he figured no one would be looking along this road if no evidence was found by the cave. Ramm turned south onto a barely visible earthen track.

He would soon cross Hyder Road, an area more populated than the land he'd passed through. He hoped the army of police helicopters wasn't already scouring the area, and that, at the moment, they had their hands full with the victims.

Twenty-minutes later, Ramm pulled the car to the edge of one of the Rowley Mine's minor shafts. Unlike the main vent, this one had been drilled straight into the earth. Originally, according to the paperwork from the Arizona Board of Mines and Minerals, the shaft was a 280-foot dead drop, though water and backfill now clogged the lower 160 feet. Still, the shaft suited Ramm's purpose.

He shifted into neutral, shut down the engine, and got out. Ramm eased the vehicle to the edge of the shaft and closed the door. Just a small push and the car bearing the bodies of Billy and Ray edged over the precipice. For a moment, the blue Chevy hung there, front tires suspended. Then the undercarriage scraped and scratched at the stone, and slid into the darkness, banging several times on the bedrock on the way down.

Ramm heard the car slap into the water. He waited, listening as air bubbled from the Chevy. When all was quiet in the inky hole, he checked the ground for evidence. Finding none, Ramm took off for home.

26

AT SEVEN A.M., the ringing phone pierced Kate Butler's brain and forced the pleasant dream to evaporate. She groped for the offensive device, her mind still gauzy with sleep, the few lingering threads of the fantasy slipping away. Kate loved to dream. She especially enjoyed when her subconscious reminded her that she was, in fact, dreaming. Then she could do anything, be anything she wanted.

The phone rang again, reminding Kate that anyone who called before nine a.m. was ill raised and downright rude. She would never be a morning person, had given up trying, but the call might be work, and she needed the money. She took a deep breath, grabbed the phone, and produced the actress.

"Good morning." She utilized the deep, throaty quality of her voice that had often been, not unkindly, compared to that of a phone-sex worker. Her tongue felt sticky. That last glass of wine might have been redundant.

"Kate, it's Jim."

She liked the Channel 10 assignment editor. His calls meant work.

"Hey!" She tossed off the down comforter, and swung her legs out of bed. "What can I do for you, Jim?"

"We're in a real bind. Can you come in?"

"Let me get my book to check my schedule," she said, knowing full well her calendar was wide open.

"Pete's out of town on his honeymoon."

Trophy bride number three, she mused.

"Sandy's got some kind of bug. And Jan's in the hospital."

"Dropping another little anchor person, is she?"

"Twins."

Kate groaned.

"We really need some help … *today*."

Kate took the phone from her ear and dropped her hand to her lap. Yes, she needed the money, but this fill-in work was seriously wounding her considerable pride. She sighed and mustered up an enthusiastic voice. "I'm yours, Jim," she answered, no hint of defeat in her voice. "Whadyagot?"

"There was a train wreck out near Hyder?"

"Hyder? Where the hell's Hyder?" Was there still a place in Arizona she had not been sent to cover a story? Kate jotted down the best route as Jim recited the directions.

"I'll e-mail over all the information we've got. Give me about five minutes. Craig's already on his way out there in the live truck. And dress down. It's open desert."

"Gee, Jim. I was planning on the blue silk Donna Karan dress and some matching four-inch spikes."

"Okay, *Sandy*," he answered, sarcastically comparing Kate to the station's current anchor queen. "Just hurry. The competition's already on the road."

"Yes, sir."

Kate hung up and padded to the bathroom wearing nothing but an extra-large Arizona Cardinals T-shirt, the week's-worth of clothes she stepped over a testament to her general lack of housekeeping skills. She splashed cold water on her face and looked in the mirror.

The reflection was not necessarily a bad one; still a forty-two-year-old was looking back. Her thick auburn hair was much darker than in her youth. Kate's mother, who bemoaned the fading of her daughter's once vibrant red hair, had casually produced a gift-wrapped bottle of Clairol on her daughter's thirty-fifth birthday, but Kate declined. Unlike most of her peers, she had yet to have even a hint of gray.

Her eyes, often said to be her best feature, were blue-green with dark brows and lashes. It was true that her nose was a little thick in the middle, the result of a childhood crash on a Jungle Gym, and her front teeth were a bit crooked and fine lines now etched the corners of her eyes and mouth. Still, the overall effect was pleasing. Kate's body was strong and sturdy despite myriad broken bones from various misadventures over the years. Certainly not the Barbie-type, Kate saw herself from the neck down as the model Botticelli envisioned when he painted *The Birth of Venus*.

Despite the imperfections she saw in the mirror, Kate was an attractive woman. Men were still sometimes captivated by her combination of looks, pluck, and brains. But this was not enough to keep her employed. Every female who plied her trade in front of a television camera had a shelf life stamped firmly on her face. Kate's had expired.

She showered, let her hair air dry, and dabbed on some make-up. She'd bring the kit and paint herself to TV standards when she got to the scene.

Kate filled a padded bottle with iced tea and ignored the dirty dishes piled in the sink. She gathered two frozen bagels, a pound bag of Oreos, and four quarts of bottled water and dropped the provisions into her backpack with her phone, voice recorder, and writing supplies. Then she downed a thick pecan chocolate chip cookie, swung the backpack over one shoulder, and headed to her truck.

The black Ford Ranger with a silver toolbox in the bed was parked in front of her East Phoenix house, a ranch-style, block home typical of the 1950s. She dumped everything in a jumble on the front passenger seat.

"Shit!" Kate went back into the house and rummaged through the mess that was her desk. Finally, she located an earpiece attached to a clear plastic spiral tube that was anchored to a clip. She coiled the long IFB cord, then headed back out to the truck.

Ψ

"Coop! Hey! Jack Cooper!"

Cooper whirled around to pinpoint the origin of the voice. "Ben! How's Lake Patrol?"

"Works for me," Ben Dryden led Cooper to a still, sheet-covered form.

"I can't understand how you can dive for dead bodies. Especially ones that have been down there a while in those murky lakes." Cooper shuddered.

"You get used to it." Dryden grinned, green eyes blazing in a permanently sunburned, freckled face. "I assume it won't gross you out too much to help me with this one. Only fatality I've seen so far. Worked for Amtrak. We didn't find him 'til a moment ago. Seems somebody covered him and moved him out of the way. I just about tripped over him."

"Stay here, Ben. I'll go and get some help."

ψ

Of the 248 passengers on the Sunset Limited, about one hundred were injured. When the first light of dawn eased into the lower Gila River Valley, most of the victims, as well as Mitchell Bates—the single fatality—had been transported to area hospitals. The majority of those who had been badly hurt arrived at St. Joseph's Hospital in Phoenix, their bodies covered with fine desert dust.

ψ

A short time after the body of Mitchell Bates had been removed, Cooper pointed toward a helicopter attempting to land. "Here they come!"

"Shit! I'm sure it's friggin' Franklin." Dryden squinted into sun that was just edging over the horizon. "How does he always get here before everybody else?"

Cooper watched the Channel 3 reporter motion to the pilot to set the chopper down.

"Who the fuck is that?"

Cooper turned and saw an FBI agent staring at the helicopter.

"No! No!" The agent waved his arms, pointing the pilot away from the wreckage. He spoke into a radio. "This is a no-fly zone. Get that news whore out of here. That's all we need. More dust stirred up."

Cooper watched the man stomp away. The copter veered off, finally settling down several hundred yards away from the wreckage.

Cooper looked at Dryden. "The rest of the idiots should

be here shortly, I'm guessing."

"Can't wait," Dryden spit into the sand.

"I guess we'd better go check the perimeters. Gotta keep our journalists properly caged." Cooper gave Dryden a mock salute.

"Hey, Coop, isn't that why you left Phoenix for that hermit lifestyle? The constant evil media horde?"

"Just one of the reasons, Ben. Just one of the reasons."

27

KATE LEFT HER PHOENIX HOME and drove east on Interstate 10. After traveling about twelve miles, she turned right onto Maricopa Road into what was one of the more unattractive areas of the Sonoran Desert. Dry dusty flatlands dominated a landscape where no appreciable rain had fallen in months, leaving the scattered vegetation pale courtesy of a coating of fine desert dust.

Periodically, Kate passed vibrant green fields, owing their effulgence to constant irrigation. She drove through the town of Maricopa, past Aida's Cafe, and a decaying billboard, announcing Jesus Christ is Lord to All. The truck raced past herds of sheep and Brangus cattle feeding on piles of stacked hay. An ungainly tangle of prickly pear growing out of the ruin of a crumbling stone house caught her attention as she flew by, as did a massive tumbleweed that struggled to free itself from a barbed-wire fence.

As Kate neared Route 8, the view became more picturesque. Thanks to a rise in elevation, giant saguaros now dotted the landscape. Bushy palo verde trees added a fine verdure to the pale hills. A couple of crosses, glowing white against the azure sky, stood boldly atop the mountain near the turnoff. A road sign announced that Kate was 326 miles from San Diego, 34 miles from Gila Bend. Another gave her permission to drive 75 miles-per-hour. Kate mashed the gas pedal settling in at 80.

Spiny ocotillo shot out of the desert floor, their spindly, thorn-covered branches rich with tiny green leaves, but this time of year the plants were free of the oddly-shaped orange blooms for which they were famous. A hawk rested on a scraggly saguaro near the asphalt, the cactus pocked by wrens, and its skin darkened by car exhaust.

The road crossed an almost endless succession of washes with peculiar names like Vekol and Sand Tank. Every so often, a small white cross—some decorated with plastic flowers and religious trinkets—appeared by the roadside, marking the place a motorist had died. Relatives believed these spots indicated the location where the soul of their loved one had officially fled the body, and so honored these places with the same enthusiasm dedicated to the victim's actual gravesite.

Just as suddenly as the attractive desert greenery appeared, the foliage vanished, leaving Kate again in a flat, desiccated wasteland. She noticed a Sandhill Crane, light gray wings spanning almost eight feet across, as the bird glided effortlessly above a dirt field that stretched into the horizon.

The road sign read *Hyder 1 Mile*. The exit was for two towns—Sentinel and Hyder—but when she exited the turnoff, Kate found herself facing little evidence of civilization. A dilapidated gas station stood on one corner, a tiny enterprise boasting two gas pumps and a backyard littered with several broken-down shacks and half-a-dozen rusting cars.

Kate quickly encountered another sign informing her she was still seventeen miles from Hyder. She continued, crossing the dry Gila River bed, past a curious field of giant, long-dead palm trees planted in neat lines, and finally to the end of the road marked by the Southern Pacific Railroad tracks.

She checked her watch. It was 11:41 a.m.

28

KATE SLAMMED ON THE BRAKES, skidded to a stop, and jumped from the truck without bothering to lock the door. She noted that all the local media outlets were clustered a good distance away from the frantic activity in the wash below. She could see their live trucks; satellite dishes perched on top, tilted at different angles depending on where their signals were being sent. The radio, TV, and print reporters mingled in a knot south of the trucks.

Kate approached the throng. A press conference was underway. What she really wanted to do was get closer to the wreck, the investigative reporter in her restless to scope out the situation, but her primary responsibility was to locate the Channel 10 live-truck driver. She checked her watch again. It was eleven forty-four.

Her heart skipped. *What if they want a live-shot for the noon news?*

"Sorry, only press allowed in this area." A hand gently grasped Kate's elbow.

She turned to see a familiar grin. "Fuck you, Coop."

"Well, if it isn't the famous Kate Butler." Jack Cooper smiled. "It's been a long time."

"What is it? Two years since you bailed out of the big city and moved here to the hinterlands? Don't you miss Phoenix?" Kate asked the former Phoenix P.D. detective.

"Not at all. Then again, out here I don't get to rub shoulders with all you media folks very often."

"I bet you sure do miss that." Kate stared at Cooper for a long moment and then looked past him. "I'd love to chat, Coop, but I think there's a live truck with my name on it in there somewhere." She nodded toward the mob of reporters and media technicians.

"Got any credentials?"

"Shit, Coop. Craig's got 'em. I didn't have time to go into the station."

"Who are you working for now?"

"Channel 10. Just filling in." She looked away.

"Where are their regular folks?"

"Sick, honeymooning, dropping babies. All that stuff normal people do." Kate checked her watch again. It was 11:46. "Give me a break. I've gotta find Craig."

"I'll have to escort you there myself." Cooper motioned to a police officer, who waved them through. Kate followed him into the media pen. "I need to make sure you're really working press."

"Damn, Cooper. You caught me. Couldn't think of a better way to spend the day than to drive out to *Hyder*." She swept an arm to take in the desert landscape. "You think they could have found an uglier location to derail a train?"

"On the contrary. There are many beautiful places out here, Kate. Allow me to show them to you. At your convenience, of course." He gazed at her.

"Never stop trying, do ya, Coop?"

"No."

Kate saw the playfulness was gone, something in his eyes. She opened her mouth to comment but was interrupted by the sound of her name being shouted.

"Kate! Kate!" Craig, the live-truck driver called frantically, waving his arms to get her attention.

The moment was lost.

"I ... I've gotta go, Coop." She turned, checked her watch again, and bolted toward the truck.

Fifteen minutes later, Kate adjusted the IFB in her ear, and clipped the coiled tubing to the back collar of her denim shirt. A hand-held microphone with a Channel 10 windscreen was wedged between her thighs. She smeared on lipstick, then smoothed her hair. Kate grabbed the mic, then the slim spiral reporter's notebook from her back pocket. She looked down at the page. *Where were her notes?*

The producer back at the station in Phoenix yelled in her ear.

"Craig! He's killing me," she said to the live-truck driver. "Turn it down. Jesus, who is this guy?"

But the cameraman didn't answer. His hand, stretched high above the camera, contracted into a fist, one finger extending. The red tally light atop the camera blinked on. He brought his arm down, and pointed at her.

Kate had neglected to get the names of the anchors in the studio. She had also missed her introduction, and so was unaware of whether they had asked her a question. So much for live television.

"Early this morning on a lonely stretch of Southern Pacific Railroad track ..."

Kate went on to give the sketchy information she had gathered. The only video available was of Maricopa County Sheriff Joe Arpaio surveying the scene. The lawman—a local celebrity—was said to be the toughest sheriff in the country for forcing inmates to wear pink underwear, serve on chain gangs, and eat green bologna. Reporters loved him for the simple fact that he was a living, breathing sound bite twenty-four hours a day. That the train wreck occurred in Yuma County and out of Arpaio's jurisdiction did not seem to bother the sheriff, who never met a microphone he didn't like.

"Thirty seconds," the over-zealous producer yelled into Kate's ear. She tried not to wince, then glanced at the monitor, and saw the video segment Craig had cut was about to end. At that moment, Arpaio conveniently sauntered within arm's reach.

Kate never hesitated. "And now with us live is Sheriff Joe Arpaio." She grabbed the lawman's shoulder, gracing him with a brilliant smile.

"Kate. Oh! Sure." The lawman blinked into the camera from behind thick glasses.

"Anything new on the cause of the wreck of the Sunset Limited, Sheriff?"

"Well, Kate, yes, there is. A letter was found that we believe was written by the person or persons who committed this heinous crime."

"Can you tell us what it said?"

"No, I'm afraid we're not prepared to release that information yet. Of course, we are coordinating with the Yuma County Sherriff's Office and the FBI."

The cameraman gave the sign to wrap up and toss back to the anchors in the studio.

"Thank you, Sheriff Arpaio." Kate faced the camera. "We'll have more on this tragedy, the wreck of the Sunset Limited, later on today. For Channel 10 News, I'm Kate Butler."

"That was great!" Craig gushed when the live-shot ended, and the sheriff had moved on.

"Got lucky. I had no idea Arpaio had just been briefed on the letter. And here's to our Sheriff, who never says no to a photo-op."

An hour later, Kate sat in the live-truck reviewing footage Craig recorded after the live shot, as well as some interviews she'd done. She charted the B-roll—jotting down shot descriptions along with their time code—so when her piece was written and ready to be edited, Craig would have an easy time identifying the proper shots to place over each section of her voice-over.

She called the station and was informed by the young, and very loud producer that they might want her to go live again during the five-o'clock news, but that she'd be free to snoop around for a while. He asked that she contact him every thirty minutes.

After Kate wrote the script for her news package, she cut the audio. She left the audio recording, sound bites, and B-roll information along with a copy of the hand-written script for Craig to edit. Then, in the hope of seeing more of the wreck site, Kate wandered to the edge of the media pen, walking the perimeter. She watched the police come and go down into the wash. Then she saw him.

"Coop!" Kate called, waving her arms.

Cooper walked over. "At your service."

"I want to see it."

"But you're media. I can't—"

"Bullshit!"

Cooper smiled. Kate was well aware that he'd always liked her brash manner. He also appreciated her honesty. Unlike a lot of younger media-types who would sell their souls for a scoop and screw the source in the process, a confidential comment with Kate stayed off the record.

"Let me see what I can do. But keep it quiet. Can't have your brethren thinking I'm playing favorites. On top of that, the FBI guys are going to be here in numbers, so bear with me."

"Thanks, Coop. I appreciate anything you can do."

"Of course, you will owe me."

Kate laughed. "Of course."

29

EARLY THAT EVENING, Kate pulled the IFB from her ear, unclipped the device, and slid the molded earpiece into her pocket. She glanced around and noted that the other TV reporters were also off the air. All the stations did stories pretty much exactly the same way, and even in the same order, give or take the cutesy fluff pieces the stations were using much more frequently these days.

Craig broke down the equipment, coiling the multiple electrical cords in neat rings before storing them in a red plastic crate. "Kate, go ahead and call in," he said. "See what they want for the ten o'clock."

Five minutes later, Kate pulled open the side door of the live truck. "Bernie said to send in all of the raw video and any unused sound bites. He's gonna have Kim cut a package, so he won't need us tonight."

"Good."

"But don't get too excited. He wants us back here first thing in the morning to do a live shot for *Daybreak*."

"Shit! There goes another night's sleep."

"Do you think they'll spring for a hotel room?" Kate dreaded the drive to Phoenix and the quick turnaround.

"Probably not. Anyway, I doubt there's a room within fifty miles of here. Look at all the people. I guarantee they've grabbed up anything even remotely nearby."

"You're probably right."

There was about an hour of daylight remaining. Kate could either get a jump-start on the drive home or try to get a little closer to the wreck. She could also ask about the letter.

After she found Cooper, he stood with his arms folded across his chest. "As far as the letter is concerned, I don't know any more than you do."

"But you've seen it, haven't you?" Kate asked.

"Them."

"Them?"

"There were four copies found. I can only assume they all say the same thing, but I haven't read them. The Feds have the letters in their white tent over there." He pointed to a large structure that had mushroomed out of the desert earlier in the day.

"They gave us a few highlights," he continued. "But, generally, peons like us local boys are welcome only if invited. And, so far, nobody's begging me to drop by for tea."

"Take me over there." Kate nodded toward the tent. "Let me see if I can finagle my way in."

"No."

She frowned, furrowing her brow like a disgruntled ten-year-old.

"But how about we take a little walk? Maybe get you just a little closer to the wreck."

Kate beamed her best smile.

"Don't get too excited. You aren't gonna be climbing on any wreckage, or touching any maimed, broken bodies, no matter how much you beg."

Kate frowned again.

"You will only go where I tell you to go. And don't talk to anyone. I know it's against your nature, but don't ask any questions. And for God's sake, take off your media credentials."

"Yes, sir." Kate slipped the cord holding her plastic credentials packet over her head and stowed the papers in her jean-jacket pocket.

"Good." Cooper walked toward the wash and Kate followed. "And, may I say, you are much more attractive as a normal person."

Kate couldn't help but smile. She'd always had a serious soft spot for Cooper and had missed him.

The broken train looked like a toy a baby giant tossed aside.

"It's gonna be a real pain getting that thing back on the track." Cooper stared at the train that remained basically intact, though some of the windows had been blown out.

"How are they going to do it?" Kate squinted at the wreckage from behind dark sunglasses.

"The heavy equipment is on the way. Though I'm not sure where they'll be able to set up the crane. It'll have to be a monster to lift those cars."

Kate itched to go down and examine the wreckage. She wanted to see inside the train, but not because she was ghoulish or sadistic, as Cooper sometimes accused her of being. She simply wanted to get a better feel for what happened, for what the victims had gone through. Kate often used small, seemingly unimportant details to color her stories, scenes that often made her pieces more poignant than those of her peers. She'd insist the videographer shoot the stuffed animal, the single shoe, the book with the interesting title, then she'd write the shot into her piece. The technique worked well, as the six Emmys for reporting that sat dust-covered on her mantel attested.

Kate unconsciously took a few steps toward the edge of the wash. She felt Cooper's hand on her shoulder.

"Oops! Sorry, Coop. Just habit. Can't help myself."

"Cooper!" They both turned to see the red-haired diver, Ben Dryden, bounding toward them.

"Hey, Kate," Ben said genuinely glad to see the reporter. Then he narrowed his eyes. "Hey, wait a minute. What are you doing out of your pen?"

"Coop deputized me."

"Oh, really?" Dryden stared at Cooper who offered a guilty shrug in return.

"Well then, Deputy Butler. Are we now off the record?"

She nodded. "Of course."

"Got a new wrinkle, kids. Seems we've got a kidnapping on our hands. A woman was taken to St. Joseph's Hospital in Phoenix with head injuries. She woke up a few hours ago and kept asking where her daughter was."

"And," Kate leaned forward, impatient to get the whole story.

"And, no one seems to know where the kid is. Though the mother insists the child would be hard to miss. She's sixteen and has some kind of facial birth defect."

"You don't think she's still on the train? Under something maybe?" Cooper scanned the wreck site.

"Nope. The train's been searched in and out. The girl's not here. And to make matters a bit more urgent, the kid is a little over eight months pregnant."

Kate mulled the facts. "All right. Where do I stand with this, Ben? Can I use anything?"

"The FBI wants to keep this quiet for now. They've begun a search, but they don't want to give the kidnapper, if there is one, any ammunition. They're waiting for him to make contact. So, for now, it's all completely off the record. I'm sorry, Kate."

Cooper wrapped his arm around her shoulders. "Sometimes, it's tough having ethics."

"Sometimes, it just plain sucks," she said.

"Hey, any chance the kid just walked off the train at some stop without momma knowing?" Kate reached to her back pocket for her pad and pen, then paused. "Notes for later. When this information is OK to use."

Dryden nodded.

"There are plenty of stops," Cooper said.

Dryden shook his head. "She got on in Hyder. The first stop was the bottom of that wash."

30

RAMM SAT SCRUNCHED in the corner of the bedroom still dressed in camouflage, knees drawn to his chest, face painted black.

"Papa?" Kelly opened her eyes, scanned the unfamiliar room, and found the apparition. She watched as he stood and stepped toward her, blue eyes glowing against the dark face. She screamed.

"No! No, Kelly! It's all right. It's Jason!"

She sucked in gulps of air. Her head pounded. "But … why do you look like that?" She backed away as he sat on the edge of the bed.

"It's nothing. I'll explain later."

"Where are we?" She tentatively touched the bump that swelled above her left cheek.

"I'll get you some ice for that." Ramm rose.

"The train. What happened to—?" Kelly was interrupted by the feel of a wet tongue on her hand. "Hello," she relaxed and scratched Dog's mottled head.

"Let me get cleaned up and make you something to eat. Then I'll tell you everything." Ramm left Kelly alone with the dog.

Later, washed and dressed in faded jeans and a light blue sweatshirt, his hair wet and slicked back, Ramm tapped on the bedroom door. "Kelly, are you awake? I've brought you something to eat."

"Yes, come in."

Kelly watched as he set a tray on the side table. He took some pillows from the closet and eased them behind her back so she could sit up.

"It's peanut butter and grated carrots on whole wheat," he said, placing the tray on her lap. "And don't say anything until you've tried it. The combination might seem a little odd, but it tastes really good. And it's very healthy." He poured hot black tea from a delicate blue and white teapot sporting dragons on the handle and spout.

Kelly picked up half the sandwich, took a bite, chewed thoroughly, and swallowed. "You're right. It's very good."

When Kelly finished her lunch, she clasped both hands above her stomach. "What happened, Jason? Why am I here?"

"This is where I live." He struggled with what he should tell her. "There was a train wreck. Not far from Hyder. I was nearby when it happened, so I went to find you."

"My mother?"

"I carried you out, but didn't see Miranda," he lied.

"Did you tell Elect Sun I was here?"

The question stung. All logic pointed to the fact that he should return Kelly to Elect Sun, but then she'd be handed over to Miranda, and the girl would be sent away again. He tried to convince himself she should not be moved yet, but Elect Peter could easily be summoned to make that diagnosis and, considering the baby, any delay in getting her to a doctor would be foolish.

But how could he explain the fact that he'd spirited the injured girl away in the darkness without drawing undue attention to himself? He remembered the two dead boys submerged in the murky water at the bottom of the mineshaft. What would Kelly think of his savage retribution. Could she understand why, with no thought of turning the other cheek, he had appointed himself judge, jury, and gleeful executioner; or might she be disgusted that he derived pleasure from making the one boy suffer?

He stared at the floor. "My phone is not working, Kelly. And I didn't want to leave you alone, so I haven't been able to tell anyone yet."

He looked up. The lie seemed to appease her, and she nodded thoughtfully. Then her eyes went wide.

"Are you all right?"

"It's just the baby. It's really kicking."

That evening, Ramm pulled a couple of thick steaks from the refrigerator and tossed them on the grill, the one he'd built, like the fireplace, with weathered bricks from the remnants of the Rowley Mine buildings. After wrapping some sweet corn in foil, he placed the ears onto the edge of the grill. A bag of frozen french-cut green beans and a loaf of Elect Sun's whole-grained bread filled out the meal.

They sat at an unpainted wooden table just to the right of the front steps, overlooking the mountains to the west. Kelly lifted another morsel of beef to her mouth, savoring the taste.

"You missed meat?"

"Yes, though it makes me feel a little bad now." She stared as Ramm ate another forkful of steak, which was blood rare.

"When I'm with the Children, I honor their beliefs," he explained between bites. "But when I'm not, I do what I think is right."

"And eating meat is right?" Kelly placed her fork on the plate.

"I think there's a reason humans have canines." He tapped one of his pointed eyeteeth.

Kelly looked down at the dog lying contentedly at her feet.

"Dog uses her sharp teeth to rip flesh," Ramm explained. "So do we. Why do we have these teeth if we are not meant to consume meat? Besides, you need meat right now. Iron and protein for you and the baby. Trust me. Elect Sun will understand."

Kelly paused for a moment, distilling the information, then picked up her fork.

By the time the sun disappeared over the horizon, leaving tendrils of magenta and apricot reaching across the desert sky, the girl had consumed every morsel of steak on her plate, and some of Ramm's, as well.

He rose to clear the table, placing the dirty dishes on the large white platter that previously held the steaks. He climbed the stairs and opened the screen door with his foot, disappearing into the cabin. The door snapped shut behind him.

Kelly, having dropped her napkin, reached to the ground to pick it up. That's when she heard the crash.

"Jason!"

She found him on his knees, the platter and dishes shattered on the pine floor. His hands were clenched in tight fists, cords bulging in his neck. Slowly, he opened his eyes. She called his name again and again, but he didn't respond.

ψ

When Ramm awoke, he was lying on the couch, a cool washcloth folded over his forehead, a green quilt draped over his body. Kelly sat in an upholstered chair, feet up on the matching ottoman. He looked away from her.

"What's wrong with you, Jason?"

"You wouldn't understand," he answered coldly.

"Why not?"

"You're a child."

"My age makes me unable to understand when someone is in pain? Is that what you mean?"

"Of course not. It's just …"

"What?"

Her odd guttural tone was beginning to sound normal. He wanted desperately to explain himself to someone, but he didn't want to frighten Kelly. She might be the one who could help him, so he couldn't risk driving her away.

Ramm took a deep breath and sat up. "I'm going to make some tea. And then I have a story to tell you."

Later, a blaze of pungent mesquite crackled in the fireplace. "I was sent on assignment to Jerusalem." He cupped his hands around a hot mug of honey-laced tea.

"The Holy Land?" Kelly took a chocolate chip cookie from the plate beside her. "Where Jesus was crucified?"

"Yes. That's right." Ramm paused. He would not tell Kelly what kind of assignment he was on, or anything about his life as an assassin, but he would tell her what happened.

ψ

When Ramm witnessed the woman sobbing before the altar at Golgotha, his immediate thought was to turn away, to leave her alone with her grief. Instead, he stood transfixed in the room that tradition declared marked the spot where Jesus allegedly hung on the cross. The woman pressed her cheek to the cold floor, tears staining the worn stone as she wailed.

As Ramm watched, he became suffused with a strange sense of calm, felt as if viscous, golden liquid now ran through him, causing a pleasant warmth. He walked toward the woman, his mind free of pain for the first time since the war.

He knelt, reached out and stroked her hair, and spoke words he had never been able to recall, but their effect mesmerized the grieving woman. After she calmed, he helped her up, and was surprised that she seemed to recognize him. The anguished sobs turned to cries of relief and, in happiness, she threw her arms around him.

Two Israeli policemen entered the room.

"Why, Mary," one said, speaking in heavily accented English. "How are you doing today?"

The policemen walked toward them and gently removed the woman's arms from around Ramm's neck.

"Sorry, sir. We'll take care of her, won't we, Mary?"

"We know just who to call." The other policeman took the woman by the hand, but she shrieked and fought him.

Not unkindly, both policemen pulled her away from Ramm, but she strained toward him.

Speechless, Ramm watched as they led her to the stairway. The woman struggled to free herself, tried mightily to keep her eyes focused on Ramm. Then all three of them disappeared around the stone corner, her cries the only thing reassuring him that he had not imagined the episode.

Alone in that sacred place, Ramm gazed at his hands. They were different. He was different. The warmth still flowed over him, around him, from him.

Suddenly, a sickening bolt of fear surged through Ramm. He turned from the altar and fled the Room of Pity. He ran past the glass mosaics, one of which depicted the outstretched body of Jesus twisted in horrifying agony on the cross.

Taking the stairs three at a time, Ramm bolted out of the Church of the Holy Sepulcher, and into the sunlight of Jerusalem's Christian Quarter.

Ramm stopped telling the story, and looked at the girl whose face, as always, remained immobile. Only her eyes could show concern. Ramm wasn't sure what he read in those eyes now. All he knew was that he was suddenly exhausted, emotionally drained.

"Kelly, do you mind if we finish this tomorrow?"

31

TEN O'CLOCK THE FOLLOWING morning, Cooper stood outside the white FBI tent that was functioning as the organization's field office. Since the media people were safely cordoned off in the pen, and he had not been issued any other specific duties, he was now unabashedly eavesdropping.

"No, sir." A tightly strung voice came from inside the tent. "Other than the letters, um ... copies of the letter, we haven't found anything."

"No tire tracks? Shoe tracks? Tools?" a deeper voice asked.

"No. The ground was completely chewed up by the helicopters and emergency crews."

Cooper slipped around to the front of the tent to get a glimpse inside. There wasn't much to see; just a few tables, chairs, and a large white board.

"Okay." The man addressing the group said. "Did we check every possible site that might have given this guy a chance to admire his handiwork?"

Cooper recognized the FBI man he'd run into the day before. He watched him pace across the front of the seated agents, hands locked behind his back, brush-cut head down as he walked.

"Beth, what have you got on the kidnapping?" he asked a butchy-looking, though not unattractive, blonde.

"No calls. No note. No contact of any kind." She responded with professional air. "The mother, Miranda Garcia, lives in Agua Caliente, just a mile or so from Hyder. Woman's poor. Lives in a three-room house. Eduardo Garcia also lives there. Says he's her husband, but there's no paperwork on a marriage. Common law, maybe."

"And the girl? What do we know about her?"

"Daughter of Miranda and Bryan Kelly. He's deceased. Vietnam Vet. Suicide. Garcia is her stepfather. It's rumored that he's the one who impregnated her."

Snickers filled the room.

"That's enough, people. Let's try to act like professionals. Beth, go chat with the mother again. See if anyone had a motive to take the kid."

"Maybe papa likes the young thing better than momma," another agent joked.

"Sure, Tom," the boss said. "And to get even, momma abducted the girl while she was unconscious. The woman was taken to the hospital, for crissakes." He pinched the bridge of his nose. "Everybody, except Frank, out of here. Find out what the hell is going on."

The other agents exited ignoring Cooper, since he was just a lowly local cop. He continued to listen to the conversation coming from inside the tent.

"Frank, we need to make a decision on the letter."

"I think we should release parts of it to the media today," Frank said. "There's nothing in the letter that's especially shocking, and maybe if we give the idiot a little press, he'll start getting a big head and brag about what he did. We don't have anything else to go on at the moment."

"Do you think the girl might have something to do with the wreck?"

"Who knows?"

ψ

At 10:30., Kate sat munching an Oreo and reviewing newly shot B-roll. She yawned, tired from the drive, since she'd returned to Phoenix the night before and then had to turn around and come right back to the wreck site.

A car pulled next to the live truck, crunching to a stop on the gravel. Kate, engrossed in the package she was composing for the noon show, didn't notice Sandy Taylor step out of her silver BMW convertible.

"Hel-loo!" Channel 10's lead female anchor, fifteen years younger than Kate with credentials consisting primarily of a stint as Miss Arizona, teetered on towering crimson heels as she tried to negotiate the uneven desert caliche. Kate noticed that the shoes perfectly matched the woman's jacket-skirt ensemble. Massive diamonds studded her ears. On the ring finger of her left hand, she waved a brilliant pear-shaped emerald surrounded by an ostentatious circle of diamonds.

"Ah, to marry well," Kate mused, thinking of her two failed legal liaisons.

"Sandy." Kate waved as the woman staggered toward her.

"I'm feeling much better now, Kate. Thanks for asking. Jim told me to tell you that we don't need you here anymore."

She removed massive designer sunglasses and graced Kate with a perfectly capped smile.

Eyeing the woman coolly and showing no emotion, Kate slipped from her perch in the live truck, ripped the notes she'd taken on the B-roll from her reporter's notebook, and placed them on the seat. She knew Sandy was incapable of putting together a story even if she had all the elements handed to her.

Craig, the live truck driver, having watched the exchange, came around to the side of the truck. "Hey, Kate. You did a hell of a job out here. I really appreciate it."

Kate forced a smile. The pity in his voice was like a physical blow. Sandy, oblivious, started jabbering about something as she leaned into the convertible and grabbed a bulging make-up case from the passenger seat.

Kate smiled as if heading off on a picnic. "See ya, Craig. Sandy." She pulled the chain holding the credentials packet over her head and dropped the documents on the seat. "Never let 'em see ya cry," she muttered, flinging her back pack over her shoulder.

A short time later, Kate sat alone on a flat rock sparsely shaded by a scrubby patch of creosote. She tossed small stones at a hefty chunk of black basalt.

"Hey! Shouldn't you be getting ready for a noon liver, or whatever it is you call those things?" Cooper asked.

She didn't answer.

He sat and began flinging pebbles along with her. After he hit the rock square on three consecutive tries, Kate finally spoke. "Can't you let me feel sorry for myself in peace?"

"Kate Butler? Winner of six Emmys and assorted other TV award-type stuff that I do not know enough about to mention specifically? That Kate Butler? Investigative reporter extraordinaire? Network workhorse? You are kidding."

Kate sighed. She couldn't help smiling. "Today the legend feels like shit, thank you very much. Didn't you know? Legend just means old. Same as pioneer. It's a nice way to say you're over the hill."

"And why does Kate Butler feel so old?"

"Sandy showed up."

"Ah. Well, of course you feel crotchety. Is she wearing those delicious spikes she's so well known for?"

Kate looked down at her favorite worn black cowboy boots and elbowed Cooper hard in the ribs.

"Just kidding." He winced from the assault. "You know I'm a boot man. Always have been. Give me a girl in a pair of cowboy boots and …"

"Nothing else?"

"Exactly. Girl of my dreams."

Kate checked her watch, a nervous habit from years of dealing with frantic TV deadlines always measured in seconds. She unhinged the timepiece and buttoned it into the top pocket of her jacket.

Then Cooper checked his watch. "Wouldn't you know it? I'm off in two hours. Do you think I could find anyone out here who'd like to have dinner with me tonight?"

Before Kate could answer, Cooper's phone rang. He looked at the electronic leash.

"You've been saved by the bell, Butler. But don't move. I've gotta call my boss."

Kate turned from Cooper and stared across the open desert that lay between her and the area filled with bustling media people. She had always enjoyed the camaraderie of her peers, back when, despite working for different news outlets, reporters helped one another if the need arose. If Channel 10's camera died at a press conference, someone at another station would make a copy of the video for Kate to use knowing at some point in the future the favor would be returned. But reporters were adversaries now, the all-for-one and one-for-all attitude having been replaced by a lot of selfish egos eager to do anything to get to the Network.

"Okay. I'll get right on it," Cooper signed off and looked at Kate.

"Right on what?"

"The boss wants me to look into the kidnapping. The FBI guys have their hands full here, and they thought since the girl is from the Hyder area, we local boys might have a little more insight into her disappearance."

"Makes sense. So, I guess this means dinner is off?"

"Absolutely not." Cooper extended a hand.

Kate grasped on and he pulled her up. She dropped the pebbles in her palm to the dirt.

As they walked back toward the media pen, Kate suppressed a smile. He was nothing if not persistent. Had been since the day she met him eight years earlier while covering a murder case. But Kate always shied away from dating cops, worried that, with her job, a boyfriend in blue could become a conflict of interest.

"I really should get back to Phoenix," she said.

"Why? You planned to be out here tonight, and I can use your help. Someone with your experience covering crimes."

"That's a bit of a stretch."

"Not at all. You ran into plenty of criminals when you were on the city beat. Seems I recall you doing a number of investigative pieces on crimes on the res, as well. Am I wrong?"

"No, those stories were on unresolved sexual assaults on Native land. They earned me two Emmys."

"That's one of the things I love about you. Your modesty."

Kate couldn't help herself. She laughed and shook her head.

"Seriously. I'm formally asking for your assistance, Kate Butler." Cooper was unwilling to let Kate slip away again. "I have some interviews to do with the girl's mother and stepfather. Drive along with me."

"Interviews? Well, that's certainly right up my alley."

He paused, a frown creasing his face. "While I hate to even ask, you're not working for any other media organization at the moment, are you?"

"No, Coop. Fear not. I am credential-less. Just an average civilian." *With no prospect of any work at the moment and nothing to go home to.* "But don't you think your boss might get just a little squirrelly knowing you're driving around with a reporter while you're on the job?"

"Let us not forget, you were officially deputized yesterday." They made their way to the white Yuma County Sheriff's Department Blazer.

"That's true."

"And besides, what Buddy doesn't know won't hurt him." Cooper opened the passenger side door. "I don't see a problem. Now get in the truck. And if you're a good girl, maybe we'll get ice cream."

Kate slugged him on the arm.

Leaving the wreck and media crews behind, Cooper turned the truck onto Hyder Road. Having Kate along on police business was not really kosher, but the Yuma County Sheriff's Office was not the Phoenix P.D. Things were a bit more laid back in the boonies. It was one of the reasons he'd given up his job in the city.

"So, did you get anything new on the kidnapping?" Kate asked.

"I learned that the mother's name is Miranda Garcia."

"The Feds gave you information?"

"No."

"You were listening in, Officer Cooper?"

"That's Deputy Cooper, missy. And no one asked me to move away from the tent. Wasn't my fault. Anyway, I just got the same information from Buddy."

"Pretty casual out here, aren't they?"

"Just the way I like it. Anyway, I was surprised. I never knew Miranda had a child."

"Miranda? You're on a first-name basis?"

"Like you said, things are casual out here. And there aren't many people. Everybody knows everybody else, or at least knows of them."

"Yet, you didn't know this woman had a child?"

"Nope. Seems odd. Though being a mother might not be something Miranda would want to advertise."

"Why not?"

"Well, she's … um …"

"What?" Kate rose one eyebrow and stared at Cooper. "Spit it out."

"She's … um … very attractive. Hispanic and Native American. Exotic. Pours well into a tight pair of jeans, and—"

"Okay. I get the picture."

After a minute of silence, Cooper spoke up. "Just so you know, I've never hit on her. Never even been introduced. I've just seen her out and about. Not my type."

"What? You don't like your women attractive and fit?"

"As a matter of fact, I do, but Miranda Garcia is reputed to be a world-class, scary bitch."

"Ah." Kate bristled at the term that had often been used in her direction. It seemed any strong, accomplished woman had to be a bitch. Maybe the appellation should be worn as a badge of honor.

"Look, Kate. When you meet her, you decide."

"Is she at the hospital?"

"She was released this morning. Her injuries are fairly minor. Her husband picked her up." He checked his watch. "And they should be home by now."

32

A BATTERED BLACK pickup rested on uneven ground in front of the fenced yard, as chickens pecked at the dirt around the vehicle's bald tires. Sea foam green aluminum siding, faded and weathered, gave the tiny house a single source of color. A cracked cement slab formed the front step.

Cooper knocked and waited. Kate stood by his side.

The door opened. A slender, handsome man of Mexican descent with dark chocolate brown eyes, smooth skin, and perfect white teeth stood before them. Despite having spent a fortune on her mouth, enough to put numerous dentists' progeny through college, Kate's teeth would never look as good as Eduardo Garcia's.

"Mr. Garcia, I'm Deputy Cooper of the Yuma County Sheriff's Office." He displayed his shield. "This is Kate Butler. May we speak with you for a few minutes? I would like to ask you some questions about your daughter."

Kate, who considered herself a master at the art of reading an interviewee, detected a change in the man's eyes at the mention of the girl.

"Of course. Please come in." Eduardo held the door open.

"Who is it?" a woman's voice called from another room.

"It's the police."

"I already talked to them. If they don't know where Kelly is, tell them to go away."

"I'm sorry," Eduardo apologized. "Miranda is feeling poorly. She hit her head in the accident."

"And I'm sure she is terribly worried about your daughter," Kate said.

"Yes, of course. Please sit." He pointed to a shabby red couch that took up much of the living room, then pulled over a straight-back wooden chair and sat before them.

"Mr. Garcia," Cooper began.

"Eduardo, please."

"Eduardo, did anyone have any reason to want to take Kelly?"

"No. No, Kelly hardly knew anyone. She was … *is* very gentle and sweet."

"Kelly has some sort of birth defect. Is that correct?"

"Yes. Her face is … different."

Kate had a hunch. "Is she competent mentally?"

Eduardo's faced creased into a frown.

"Did she attend school?" Kate said before he had a chance to answer.

Eduardo shook his head.

Kate looked at Cooper and stood. "Thank you, Mr. Garcia. We'll be in touch."

Cooper, surprised to be cut short, followed Kate out into the yard. Suddenly, the front door flew open behind them and bounced hard off the aluminum siding. Miranda stood unsteadily in the doorway exuding a wobbly, but haughty air. Disheveled, raven-colored hair swarmed over her shoulders giving her that just-got-out-of-bed look. Kate wondered if somewhere in the woman's distant past there was a royal ancestor or two. She certainly demanded attention like some sort of spoiled princess.

"You want to know where my daughter is?" Miranda shrieked. "Go talk to that stupid religious woman. She's the one who wanted to take Kelly from me."

"You mean Elect Sun?" Cooper asked.

"You ask her. Go ask that freak!"

Eduardo reached out and tried to guide Miranda back inside.

She wrenched her arm away.

"Thank you for your help," Cooper said. "We'll look into it."

As they drove out of the yard, Kate asked, "Elect who?"

"Elect Sun," he answered curtly. Perhaps he'd made a mistake bringing Kate along. "They use the title Elect to signify that they are God's chosen people. Think of it like a nun; Sister So-and-So."

"*They*. Who are they?"

Cooper ignored her question. "Do me a favor, Kate. Don't end my interviews for me. I'll let you know when we've asked enough questions."

"Got ya, chief." Kate had overstepped her bounds. But she was used to running interviews. Hadn't even given a second thought to jumping on Cooper's turf. Still, she didn't apologize.

Five minutes later, Cooper turned the Blazer down a dirt road lined with towering date palms. A wooden sign, once brightly painted in rainbow colors but now faded, proclaimed *The Children of Light—on Land of God's Ownership*.

"Where are you taking me?" Kate watched as the house at the end of the lane came into view. "Jesus, Coop."

"Exactly."

"Exactly what?"

"Jesus."

"Quit playing games. Where the hell are we?"

"Hell is very off target." Cooper eased the truck to a stop on the gravel and switched off the ignition. "This is the compound of the Children of Light."

"I got that much from the sign." Kate stared at the sprawling ranch house surrounded by an orchard of citrus trees and shaded by a towering cottonwood.

Cooper turned to face her. "The Children are waiting for the Second Coming."

"Really? And will that be sometime soon? Because I have some bills due, and it would certainly be nice not to have to worry about paying them. Also, I'd like to make some plans so I'll be ready for Armageddon. Now there's a story I'd like to cover."

Cooper was silent for a full count of ten. "Listen, Kate. Don't be such an ass. These are nice people. Nobody said you have to subscribe to their beliefs, but I won't allow you to be rude to them. They are old and kind, and if you can't be polite, you can wait here while I talk to them."

"Shit, Coop. I'm just an old recovering Catholic. On the 12-step program. Religion doesn't always bring out the best in me. It's a knee-jerk reaction that I'm truly working on. But when you've been smacked by a sadistic nun or two, it's hard to take any of that power and glory and loving God stuff too seriously. Trust me, I'm much more tolerant of believers than I used to be."

Cooper rolled his eyes. "Sorry I jumped on you."

"Let's go meet the Children." Kate reached for the door handle. "I promise I'll be on my best behavior."

Elect Peter met them at the door. "Deputy Cooper. Please come in." He led them into the living room, which Kate was surprised to see was dominated by a timeworn upright piano and a drum set. A tall, silver-haired woman with a patrician bearing and blue-gray eyes introduced herself as Elect Sun.

"Have you come about Kelly?" she asked after the introductions.

"Then you know?" Cooper held his cap in his hands.

"That she's missing? Yes. We called the information line that was posted by the authorities as soon as we heard about the accident. They said nobody by Kelly's name or description was on any of the injured lists."

"Are you sure she got on the train?"

"Yes, Deputy Cooper. I took her to Hyder Station myself. Watched her get on the train with her mother." Elect Sun's voice broke. "She waved at me from inside the car."

"We just came from Miranda Garcia's home. I have to tell you, Elect Sun, she seems to think you took the girl."

The woman stood stunned by the accusation. Elect Peter moved to her side and placed his arm protectively around her shoulders.

"Please understand. I don't believe you had anything to do with Kelly's disappearance. I just thought you should know what Miranda is saying."

Elect Sun nodded. "We just want what's best for Kelly and her baby. She's been living with us for the past few months. Miranda no longer wanted her because … because …"

"Eduardo Garcia is the baby's father," Kate finished for her.

"Yes," Elect Sun said. "And we would be happy to have Kelly live with us. Her child, as well. But Miranda wants to be rid of her. She claimed she was sending the girl to her sister in Los Angeles, but no one around here has any memory of Miranda ever having a sister. God knows where she was really shipping Kelly off to."

Kate and Cooper eyed one another, but said nothing.

"We want her to stay with us until she's old enough to go out into the world on her own," Elect Peter explained. "We want to educate Kelly. We've been working on her reading skills since she's been here."

"She's sixteen and doesn't read?" Kate said. "Is she mentally handicapped?"

"No, I don't think so. But she hasn't ever attended school. She has a facial deformity, which combined with other symptoms, is called Moebius Syndrome," Elect Peter explained. "She can't physically express herself like you would. She can't smile or frown, because she's missing certain muscles in her face, or the ones she has don't function properly. But there's nothing wrong with her mind. She's just never had anyone take an interest in her education."

"Why not?" Cooper asked.

"You know Miranda, Deputy Cooper." Elect Sun frowned. "She seems to think Kelly is ugly. Finds it difficult to believe she produced what she sees as an unattractive child. From what the girl's told us, only Bryan Kelly was ever kind to her."

"Bryan was her biological father?" Kate asked.

"Yes," Elect Peter answered. "He killed himself about eight years ago. When he came back from Vietnam, he seemed all right despite his wounds. But he began to drink. Then he started passing out regularly. He also had Agent Orange poisoning. Eventually, he couldn't hold a job. He just kept getting weaker and developing more medical problems. They say he would have ended it much sooner had it not been for Kelly."

"He's buried out in the old Pioneer Cemetery," Elect Sun added.

"There's something I don't understand," Kate said, changing tack. "How, in this day and age, in this country, can a child exist who doesn't go to school? Don't the authorities come and ask why she's not enrolled?"

"We live just a few miles from Kelly's home," Elect Sun explained. "And until a few months ago, we had no idea she existed."

"Her mother kept her locked up?" Cooper asked.

Elect Peter shook his head. "No, it wasn't like that. I think Miranda just didn't want to advertise the fact that she had a child who was different. Kelly mostly stayed home or wandered in the nearby desert. And there aren't that many people out here."

"Folks tend to mind their own business." Elect Sun slumped into a chair. "If they ever saw Kelly, they were probably put off by her face and ignored her."

Elect Peter sighed and shrugged. "She just fell through the cracks."

"So who would want to take her?" Kate asked. "Here's a kid nobody even knows, yet someone went to the trouble of kidnapping her from a wrecked train."

"We've been struggling with that." Elect Peter glanced at Elect Sun. "We don't know."

"Does she have any friends at all?" Kate inquired.

Elect Sun looked like she wanted to say something, but held back.

"No friends," Elect Peter answered. "But she did have a problem with a boy recently."

"Who?" Cooper asked.

"We don't know his name. But he tried to sexually assault her."

"Did you report it to the police?" Cooper asked.

"I'm afraid we didn't," Elect Sun admitted. "She wasn't harmed and no one knew the boy. We didn't want her to go through any more trauma, especially with the baby. You understand, don't you Deputy Cooper?"

Kate knew that he didn't. He and Kate had both attempted to interview rape victims over the years who wanted to remain silent, allowing the perpetrator to attack others. But this was not the time to fight that battle.

"We are just grateful Jason came along and rescued her."

"Who is Jason?" Kate and Cooper asked in unison.

33

RAMM SLEPT FITFULLY and, despite the aroma of fresh coffee and bacon, awoke groggy and agitated. He pushed himself off the couch, showered, dressed, and walked barefoot into the kitchen where he found Kelly had already prepared breakfast.

"Smells great," Ramm forced a smile. "I didn't know you could cook."

"I always cook at home. My mom doesn't like to, but my stepfather and I both enjoy cooking. He taught me."

Ramm sat at the table. Kelly ceremoniously placed a platter of scrambled eggs, bacon, and French toast with maple syrup before him. She produced an empty glass from the cupboard and poured fresh-squeezed orange juice from a white pitcher.

"Aren't you having any?" he asked when she sat facing him at the table with only a glass of juice.

"I ate a long time ago. While you were sleeping. Are you feeling better today?"

"Yes," he lied. "Much better."

A cool breeze laced through the open window. Kelly tilted her head. "Maybe a walk would be good."

Later that day, Ramm, Kelly, and Dog took the easy trail that led past the main Rowley Mine shaft and down into the soft, sandy wash. They made progress slowly, owing to Kelly's pregnancy and Ramm's general malaise, stopping numerous times along the way; once to watch a darting hummingbird, his crimson collar fiery in the sunlight as he busied himself gathering nectar from the tubular red flowers of a chuparosa.

Ramm watched the girl. The baby was due soon, but he had no fear for Kelly. He'd witnessed women in Vietnam bring children into the world without so much as a whimper. While Kelly was small, she was fit and strong, and if there were any problems, he could use his medical training to help.

Perhaps, he rationalized, there was no real need to quickly return her to Miranda. The woman obviously didn't want Kelly around. Wouldn't it be better to let her have the baby among friends?

A jackrabbit burst from behind a slab of fractured white quartz. Dog yelped and bolted, but with only three good legs she was no match for the hare, which darted back and forth, finally ducking into a fall of boulders at the base of a basalt mound.

"I'm a little tired, Jason. Can we rest for a few minutes?"

"Sure." Ramm motioned toward a soft, shaded spot beneath a palo verde tree, delicate, yellow-green leaves masking thorns running the length of every branch. He dropped to the ground cross-legged and held out his hand to help her. Dog returned, breathing heavily, sans rabbit, and nudged between them. A lizard skittered through the sand leaving minute markings that resembled cuneiform.

Ramm pointed to a blue butterfly—tiny wings glimmering like foil—perched on a golden wildflower that had forced its way through a miniscule crack in a flat piece of mottled rhyolite. A refreshing breeze, the first cool hint following the doggedly hot summer months, pushed at the palo verde, and created an undulating pattern on the sand.

Kelly broke the quiet between them. "What happened after you ran out of the church?"

Ramm hesitated. A calm had come over him. There was peace here with her. A fragile vacuity. As if his past deeds had drained out of him. He wanted to stay very still in the hope the horrors would not return.

Kelly turned her face up to him.

He stared back. "After the church? Things got very strange."

Ramm bolted into the street. Harsh Jerusalem sunlight startled him after the musty darkness of the church. He ran without thinking, turned down the narrow alleys. Then, out of breath, he stood beneath a long stone archway. At the end of the tunnel, shielded from the bright daylight, he pressed his forehead to the cool, pitted stone. He felt like he was disappearing—not his physical being, but the part that made him who he was. He struggled to hold on, but questions kept sounding. What had he done to benefit anyone? What positive contribution had he made? Was he someone the world really needed?

Approaching voices alarmed him, but Ramm was unable to turn from the coolness of the wall. He recognized many of the Hebrew words; enough to sense the men were having an enthusiastic argument on a miniscule point in the Torah.

They were speaking softly now, to him. Could they help in some way? Gently, they turned him from the stone. He faced two bearded, black-frocked Hasidim, polite concern in their dark eyes.

Ramm was touched by their compassion, but then he recognized the face. His senses snapped back, he recalled following the man to the cafe and remembered the plan.

Slowly, surreptitiously, Ramm reached for the concealed blade. He would have to kill them quickly.

The Hasidim, one on each side, helped him walk through the archway. His mind raced. Ramm calculated the act and his avenue of escape. Then he sensed a presence behind him, but saw no one. Sunlight loomed ahead. Ramm released his grip on the knife and ripped his arms from the men, toppling one onto the uneven cobblestones. He stood rooted to the ground, unable to run.

The target faced him, showing no fear. "Let me help you, sir," the old man said in heavily accented English. He edged closer to Ramm, arms extended, palms up.

Two Israeli soldiers approached, Uzi submachine guns slung loosely across their backs.

"Come. You need to rest," the target insisted. "We will help you." He nodded toward the soldiers, who had been talking and laughing when they entered the archway, but who were now approaching quietly.

The target reached out and took Ramm's hand in a grasp that was cool and surprisingly strong for one so old. Then Ramm felt the warmth flowing into him again. It ran like thick honey up his arm. He was tempted to pull away, but soon the sensation *moved into his shoulder, up his neck, down into his chest. The warmth filled him, and smothered the thickly layered pain that had burned within him for so long.*

ψ

In Ramm's telling of the story, he did not refer to the man as his target, had intentionally left out any mention of his real purpose in Jerusalem.

"Why were you afraid of the old man?" Kelly carefully removed a small ball of cholla needles from Dog's dense fur.

"I'm not exactly sure."

"Maybe you were sick. Sometimes I get the flu, and it makes me feel really bad, and I get frightened. And if I'm really sick, sometimes I get confused."

"Yeah. And that's exactly what the police thought."

ψ

"We saw him a few moments ago at the altar," one of the Israeli police officers said to the old Hasid who was still holding Ramm by the hand. "He was up there with Mary."

"Ah, it is strange how this happens." The man nodded. He looked at Ramm, who was no longer struggling to get away, who now had an otherworldly expression of complete serenity.

"We will send him where we send all the others," the police officer said. "He'll be fine in a few weeks."

Ramm, gently guided by the policemen, was led out of the stone archway into the brilliant light of the Jerusalem afternoon. The old man and his friend parted ways with them when the road intersected a narrow alleyway.

"Be well," the target called. His brown eyes met Ramm's before he turned the corner and disappeared.

A short time later, Ramm was handed over to a soft-spoken woman in a complex that had once been an Arab village. The stone houses of Kfar Shaul were surrounded by a wall that also enclosed sprawling gardens and hundreds of fruit trees. Crabapple, pomegranate, and fig joined a riotous array of flowers perfuming the air. Outside the wall, and beyond the twisting garden pathways of what was probably the most exotic psychiatric hospital in the world, was a drab, industrialized section of Jerusalem.

Ramm was escorted to an impeccably clean, sunny room with white wooden shutters on the windows. A nubby white spread covered the bed. An oil painting of daffodils and Queen Anne's lace hung over a bureau. A different woman appeared with two large white towels and a washcloth.

"Sir, I've drawn a warm bath for you," she said in accented English. "Please take as long as you'd like. There are fresh, clean clothes you can change into. You can leave what you're wearing on the bed. We will lock up your valuables and have your clothes washed. And, when you're ready, the doctor will see you."

The woman, an Arab with beautiful dark hair and almond-colored skin, smiled and left him alone in the room.

Ramm stepped into the sunlight that streamed through the window. He could see the gardens below and the colorless, utilitarian warehouses beyond the walls. He opened the shutters and reached to the sill, wanting to lift the window, so he could smell the perfumed air he'd noticed when he arrived. It was bolted shut.

Sitting on the bed, Ramm slowly removed his clothes. When he was naked, he placed his knife and the soft leather belt bearing his money and passports on top of the pile. Then he rose, walked into the bathroom, and eased himself into the steaming bath.

Two hours later, Ramm was escorted to a different room.

"I am Dr. Yair Bar El. Who are you?" The doctor waited for an answer.

Ramm turned to him. *"Don't you know who I am?"* he said softly.

Bar El smiled. *"I think you should tell me."*

Ramm found it difficult to speak. A small part of him fought what was happening. He walked to the window in the comfortable, well-appointed room that was Bar El's office.

"It's beautiful here. Peaceful." Something deep within him noted that the first-floor room did not have the windows bolted shut.

Bar El observed the man before him, then spoke in a calm measured tone. *"Normally, my patients come in with their identities established: the real ones and the ones their psychosis has imposed upon them. But you are traveling with numerous sets of identification papers, and no friends or relatives, concerned about the nature of your strange behavior, have come for you. There are also other issues: the matter of the knife and the large amount of cash you are carrying, money in large denominations and various types of international currency."*

Ramm stared out the window and did not respond.

"If you don't wish to tell me your name or anything about yourself, then you leave me no choice but to talk about myself." The doctor settled into one of a pair of brown leather, wingback chairs. *"I was born in Buenos Aires. Since 1982, I have specialized in treating people who are suffering as you are now."*

Ramm turned to face Bar El. *"What makes you think I'm suffering?"*

The doctor smiled. "You have an affliction we call the Jerusalem Syndrome."

When Ramm didn't respond, Bar El continued. "We get almost forty cases a year. Most of them come from North America. The vast majority are fundamentalist Protestants. By your accent, you are American. Are you Pentecostal, as well? Perhaps you were traveling with a group from somewhere in the United States?"

Ramm smiled sadly, then suddenly had a moment of complete clarity. "Doctor, I need to leave here. I have a job to finish."

"What type of job?"

Images attacked him. Ramm saw his hands wrench a young Vietcong's neck, cracking the vertebrae in one quick jerk. Through the sight of an automatic rifle, he watched blood sprout from the forehead of a Nicaraguan rebel leader. Wielding a knife, he sliced across a beautiful woman's pale throat, her eyes staring in disbelief as he dropped her twitching body into the dark river below.

A spasm wrenched the visions away. Ramm gazed into the garden. "I'm here to save mankind. When may I leave?"

Two days later, Ramm met with Bar El again.

"The medication you've been taking is called Haloperidol," the doctor explained. "It's an antipsychotic drug and, given time, it will cure you completely. Now, do you think you're ready to tell me who you are? Someone is probably worried that they haven't heard from you. We do have the police checking all missing person's reports."

Fear surged through Ramm.

When Bar El received no answer, he placed his pad and pen on the desk. "Let's go for a walk. I'd like you to meet some of the others who are staying with us."

Ramm accompanied Bar El on the path that wound among the limestone buildings, through scented gardens, past burbling fountains that played gentle, soothing music. They saw a woman grieving, her face drawn in sadness. Bar El stopped to speak with her.

Ramm recognized Mary from the church, though she seemed to have no memory of their meeting.

"She says she's the Virgin Mary," Bar El explained.

A man appeared, blond, wild-eyed, hands on his hips as he talked to no one. "Plead my cause, O Lord, with those who strive with me! Fight against those who fight against me!"

Bar El patted the man on the shoulder, but he continued his recitation of Psalm 35, ignoring the doctor.

"King David." Bar El stared at Ramm.

As they made their way through the gardens of Kfar Shaul, Ramm was introduced to three Marys, a King David, two Gods, one man who claimed to be Satan, and three Messiahs, all of whom believed they were Jesus Christ come to save the world.

34

"COOPER!" The police radio on the Blazer's dash blared.

"Buddy, what's up?"

"Get back out to the wreck site. The FBI folks have some information that might help you with the kidnapping. Check in with a guy named Pat Sanders."

"Thanks, will do."

Kate watched the headstones of the Pioneer Cemetery slide by. "I still can't figure out how they got away with keeping the girl out of school all these years."

"Kids are always slipping through the cracks. And it's not just in rural places like this." Cooper waved his hand. "I saw plenty of children, some homeless, some not, who never got an education or medical care right in the middle of Phoenix. Understaffing is rampant at Child Protective Services. Those people have caseloads way over the national average, and kids get lost all the time."

"I guess you're right. And when you're dealing with a parent who doesn't want the kid to go to school—or even go out in public—what are you going to do?"

"And let's remember, here in Arizona, which we sometimes refer to as the Mississippi of the West, people are always trying to eliminate taxes. That makes our social services situation even worse." Cooper drove north past the rows of withered palms.

"What's with the trees?" Kate gestured toward the pitiful looking plants.

"Those have been here for years. You'd think a good monsoon wind would have blown them down by now. They were going to plant them around the Hotel Modesti. That's the dilapidated building we just passed. It's where the hot springs used to be. Quite famous in its day."

"You mean people came out here to take the waters? I think that's the old expression."

The last of the desiccated palms disappeared from view.

"Yep, there was a health resort right here. The water was supposedly good for everything from skin problems to stomach ailments. They even had a masseur who worked on the guests."

"Just being away from the usual grind probably made them feel better," Kate said. "And a massage. That can never hurt."

"At your service, anytime." Cooper grinned.

Kate rolled her eyes. "You know what I mean. There's nothing sexual about a good massage."

"Of course, there isn't." Cooper feigned hurt. "You totally misunderstood."

"Right. Anyway, what happened to the springs?"

"They dried up." He turned onto Hyder Road. "Though it might be hard to believe looking at it now, this area used to be one of the most fertile valleys in the state. But too much crop irrigation, grazing livestock, and the building of the Coolidge and Roosevelt dams destroyed the water table. And when the springs disappeared, people stopped coming."

Kate examined the passing landscape: scraggly saguaros, twisted stumps of long-dead trees, and rangy mesquite and creosote scattered among the mounds of dark basalt. It was hard to believe this had once been a verdant paradise.

The Blazer pulled to a stop just outside the white FBI tent. Cooper and Kate got out and walked inside. A meeting was in progress.

"All right. Stay on it, everybody. Something's gotta break." The man in front of the group, Pat Sanders, turned to some papers on a table before him.

The agents rose from their seats and moved toward the door. After they were gone, Cooper and Kate approached.

"Agent Sanders. I'm Deputy Cooper. This is Kate Butler. I was told you have some information on the kidnapping that might be useful to our investigation."

"Cooper? Yea. Right. I do." He walked to a table that was covered with a topographical map of the area. He picked up a notebook. "We interviewed just about everyone on the train. Of course, initially, we didn't know anyone was missing. But we contacted the passengers and crew again, and found some people you might want to talk to."

"Who?" Kate asked.

Cooper shot her a warning glance.

Sanders smiled at Kate, not the least bit offended by her impatience. Had he realized she was a reporter, he might have thought differently. "Let's sit. Coffee?"

When the three of them gripped Styrofoam cups, sipping hot coffee in various shades and sweetness, Sanders continued. "Several people recall seeing a tall man. We don't think he was a passenger. They told us he came out of the desert and climbed onto the train. Most people were frightened and trying to get off. That's why they remember him. They said he appeared to be looking for something."

"Or someone," Cooper said.

"He deliberately moved past people who were asking for help. He was seen in several cars, always methodically searching. A nurse, Gretchen Howell, out of Albuquerque, described him as Caucasian, tall, thin but muscular. She thinks his eyes were light blue, but it was dark."

"Hair?" Kate asked.

"Sandy blond. No facial hair," Sanders answered.

"Do you think he might have something to do with the wreck?" Cooper asked.

"Don't know about that," the FBI man said. "But we've eliminated the only other suspects we found. Just two guys out here drinking around a campfire when it happened. They came over to check it out, but panicked and ran. Thought this might be a crime scene. One's on parole. Made him nervous. We caught up with them later. They're clean."

"So that leaves us with the tall man." Cooper tapped his finger on the table. "Is there any way to tie him to Kelly Garcia?"

"Glad you asked." Sanders consulted his note pad. "Here it is. Kid out of Tucson. Jimmy Collins. Student. University of Arizona. Said he saw the man and helped him get an injured girl out of one of the railcars that was on its side in the wash. He thought the girl looked Hispanic. He wasn't entirely sure. But he said she was very pregnant."

"Bingo." Cooper looked at Kate.

"Collins told us the girl was unconscious and that the guy ran off with her cradled in his arms."

35

A CRASHING SOUND startled Kate and Cooper, drawing their attention to the FBI tent's opening, and abruptly ended the conversation. Only Sanders didn't seem surprised.

"What was that?" Kate asked.

"Come on," the FBI agent said. "I'll show you."

The huge crane stuck high into the cloudless desert sky, cables swinging empty in the cool breeze.

"One down. Three to go." Sanders pointed at the railroad car that had just been positioned on the track.

They watched as a dozen agents streamed into the wash to scan the area below where the car had rested just moments before. Working their way through the area, they sifted through debris; tagging and bagging anything they found that might prove to be evidence.

As Cooper, Kate, and Sanders observed from the hillside, another man approached holding a manila envelope.

"Thanks." Sanders dismissed the agent and opened the package.

Cooper and Kate peeked over and saw the words Operation Splitrail on top of the first page. As Sanders perused the information, Cooper and Kate observed the workers as they hooked one of the prostrate cars to the crane's cables.

Sanders sighed audibly.

"Anything new?" Cooper kept his eyes on the activity in the wash.

"Not a whole lot. We've had almost a hundred agents scouring every inch of land within several miles of here, looking for anything that might give us a clue as to who did this. But we haven't come up with a single footprint, tire track, soda can, or anything that might have been left behind by the creep. Or creeps, as the case may be."

Kate examined the investigation below, some agents on their hands and knees as they inched across the sand. "Is that unusual?"

"It is. Militia types are not usually real meticulous," Sanders explained. "On top of that, they typically want credit for their actions."

"You're convinced this is a militia crime? Some kind of domestic terrorism?" Cooper asked.

"The letter certainly points that way. Though I've never heard of the Sons of Gestapo."

"Neither have I." Cooper turned to Sanders. "Do you think we could get a copy of the letter, to see if we can come up with a local connection?"

"Sure. I'll have one copied for you. You're more familiar with the people out here. You'd be doing us a favor. By the way, we're expecting some help from our linguistics specialists in Washington. They're studying the grammar, syntax, spelling, vocabulary. That kind of thing. They should be able to tell us something about the writer's personality, beliefs, and background by studying the words that were used."

"It's the motive I'm curious about," Kate said as the crane slowly righted one of the fallen railcars. "I mean, why do this? Why derail a train? Why this train? Why here?"

Cooper answered. "Well, there's no one around here for long stretches of time. That's a plus, I guess, if you're planning a derailment."

"And did the girl have something to do with it? Where was she going eight-months pregnant? Maybe there's a disgruntled lover involved." Kate shook her head.

Cooper watched the silver crane lift a car slowly into the air. "Eduardo Garcia fathered the child. That's the stepfather. Obviously, the mother, Miranda, was upset about it. But she was on the train, too."

"Something isn't right here," Sanders said. "But one thing is certain. The guy who planned this knew exactly what he was doing. He had the right equipment, and knew exactly what hardware to remove and where. Even how to reconnect the signal wires."

"A disgruntled railroad employee?" Kate asked.

"Wouldn't surprise me in the least," Saunders said. "We're running a check on current and former Southern Pacific employees right now. Anyone who's been fired or quit in the last five years."

"Anyone like that living out here, Coop?"

The railcar dangled silently, looking like a toy at the end of a child's pull rope.

"Nope. Can't think of anyone offhand. By the way, have you had much action on the toll-free number?" Cooper asked Sanders.

"Hardly any. We established the hot line as soon as the news broke. In the first twenty-four hours, we only got a hundred and thirty calls. And remember, about ninety-nine percent of them are bogus."

"Seems like a lot of calls to me," Cooper said.

"During the same period after the Oklahoma City bombing, we got about three thousand."

"I see your point. Then again, that was a city. This is …"

"Nowhere," Sanders said. "No offense."

"None taken. We'll check around with the locals. See what we can find."

"I'd appreciate that," Sanders said. "Come on. I'll get you a copy of the letter."

Kate opted to wait and observe the action in the wash. She watched as the railcar dropped solidly onto the track, saw the workers give the thumbs up to the crane operator. She wished she could go down and get her hands dirty with the agents sifting through the debris, searching for clues.

Cooper jogged back. "Look at that," he said, checking his watch. "Almost quitting time."

She had successfully stalled Cooper about dinner. But her time was up. Kate didn't want to go home. There was nothing there. Even Freddy, her beloved mongrel put down six months earlier at fourteen, was gone.

"You cooking?" she asked.

"Absolutely."

36

A CHILLED BREEZE WASHED over Kelly. She hugged herself. The cotton dress was thin and in need of washing.

"You're cold." Ramm rose from his seat beneath the palo verde, reached down, grasped her small hand, and helped Kelly to her feet. They began the short hike back to the cabin.

"So, were you ill?" Kelly asked as they negotiated the dirt path.

"I suppose Dr. Bar El would say so." He looked away and saw a bank of dark clouds building on the horizon.

"Are you sick now?"

Ramm rubbed one hand across the light-colored stubble that covered his jaw. "I'm not sure."

They continued the walk to the cabin in silence.

Later that evening, Kelly reclined on the couch dressed in a maroon and gold Arizona State University sweatshirt and a matching pair of pants. The outfit was too large for her, so she had rolled the waist over several times and cuffed the legs. Though the clothes appeared ungainly, they were warm, comfortable, and clean.

Ramm entered the room with a tray bearing a pot of hot tea, two cups, and a plate of homemade chocolate chip cookies direct from the freezer.

"These would be very good with ice cream," Kelly said, after biting into one of the cookies. "My favorite is mint chocolate chip."

"Sorry, no ice cream. But I'll see what I can do. First, though, we need to get you some clothes." Ramm eyed her ensemble.

"My suitcase was on the train. All my things were in it. Do you think I might get it back?" Her father's Silver Star had been packed into the front zipper pocket.

"We'll see if we can find it."

Kelly sipped her tea. Her eyes kept wandering to the sprightly creature that danced across the front of the sweatshirt. "Who is this?" She pointed at the happy looking demon.

Ramm smiled. "That's Sparky, the Arizona State Sun Devil. He's the university's mascot."

"A mascot?"

"A symbol. One that belongs to a school. When people see the Sun Devil, it makes them think of Arizona State. A mascot is usually part of the school's sports program."

Kelly appeared to mull this information over. She reached for another cookie.

"Does this mascot, this Sun Devil, do anything?"

"Well, there's a man who gets dressed in a red-colored costume with horns and a tail and a pitchfork. He runs around at games, making people laugh, and getting the fans to cheer for their team. But, generally, mascots are just symbols."

Kelly nodded her head. "Like Jesus."

"What do you mean?" Ramm asked, taken aback by her response.

"Jesus is the symbol of the Catholic Church. It bothered me when I first saw him at Mass. He looked so sad hanging on the cross. All those thorns sticking in his head. My papa said he was the symbol of the church."

Ramm didn't know how to respond.

"And before Jesus died, he went around doing things to make people happy. Like healing the sick. Papa told me he even brought dead people back to life." Kelly sat back, sipping her tea, apparently content with her correlation.

"I see what you mean." Ramm scratched his head. How might the Pope react to such a statement? The leader of the Catholic Church had once spoken at Sun Devil Stadium, but only after a heated debate about the university's mascot. Finally, it was agreed that the cartoon devil—whose visage appeared on the stadium turf and the scoreboard—would be covered so as not to offend the pontiff and his party.

"Now, tell me about a university." Kelly poured herself another cup of tea from the blue and white dragon pot.

"It's a school. A very large school with lots of students."

"I've never been to any school."

For the first time since meeting Kelly, Ramm detected a hint of self-pity in her voice. "I don't see any reason why you couldn't go to school. Maybe, after the baby is born, we can work something out."

She looked at him. "Does that mean I will be staying here with you?"

The question hung between them. Ramm felt a sudden surge of guilt. Elect Sun must certainly be frantic with worry. How could he treat her this way after the kindness she had shown him? Miranda might even be worried about the girl, though he doubted it. *Why wasn't he willing to let the girl go?*

"I don't know what we should do," he said.

"I don't either."

Kelly slept in the giant sweat suit. Ramm pulled the quilt over her bulging belly and tucked her into his bed. When was she due? He promised himself he would contact the Children first thing in the morning. Not only to assuage his guilt over causing them to worry, but also to have Elect Peter available to help the girl through the birth, in case there was no time to get her to a medical facility.

Carrying sheets, a pillow, and a star-pattern quilt, he left to make his bed on the couch.

"Jason." Kelly called as he was closing the door. "How long were you in that hospital in Jerusalem?"

"Only about five days." He answered without looking at her.

"Good." She patted the side of the bed, giving Dog permission to join her. The animal hopped up, turned around twice, and snuggled in beside her. "You must have been okay if the doctor let you out."

Ramm turned to leave, but paused in the doorway. "He didn't let me out, Kelly. I escaped."

The fire had disintegrated to burning embers, but Ramm had neither the energy nor the desire to get up and throw on another log. He kept thinking about the others being treated at Kfar Shaul. The Mary convinced she was perpetually pregnant, unable to deliver her make-believe baby, fearing the world was too evil a place for God's child. The Jesus who repeatedly called the Israeli police to report nonbelievers. And the Canadian who wept constantly because no one believed he was Sampson.

Ramm had researched the Jerusalem Syndrome in an effort to understand the condition and why it plagued him. Most of the afflicted had histories of psychiatric disorders. The vast majority of those without previous psychiatric problems were Protestants from fundamentalist homes mainly in rural sections of the United States and in Scandinavia. These people, who spent large amounts of time reading the Bible, had no system of saints or a papacy to stand between them and God. Their rituals were designed to get the believer face-to-face with the Creator, and their religious energies became concentrated on the imaginary celestial Jerusalem and the spiritual Jesus Christ. Doctors theorized that when faced with the real Jerusalem, filled with shopping malls, traffic jams, and modern businesses—a picture horribly contrary to their preconceived notion of the city—they were stricken by an acute psychotic reaction.

Most of the afflicted who had suffered no prior psychiatric disorders, recovered with the help of medication and rest and returned home too embarrassed to mention what had happened to them in the Holy City. The ones with preexisting mental conditions were not cured so easily, but were, for the most part, harmless. On rare occasions, however, the disorder proved to be dangerous. The most infamous person stricken with the syndrome was David Koresh, who recognized what he believed to be his own divinity on a visit to Jerusalem in the summer of 1983. Ultimately, Koresh and his Branch Davidian followers were killed in a standoff with federal authorities in Waco, Texas in 1993.

37

"IT'S NOT EXACTLY what I expected," Kate admitted after a brief tour of the house.

Cooper crossed his arms firmly over his chest. "All cops are slobs? Their main source of nutrition is provided by Dunkin' Donuts? And they couldn't find a hamper with a magnifying glass? Is that it? My goodness, Ms. Butler. I never thought you'd be one to indulge in stereotypes."

"Well, no. I don't, generally. But you have to admit the Waterford Crystal collection is a little out of the ordinary."

"Why? I think it's tastefully done. Just six pieces and a set of Colleen pattern highball glasses." He opened the doors of the antique barrister bookcase that housed the expensive glass. "And two pieces were gifts."

Kate giggled, which she hadn't done in a long time. "I was wondering how you'd buy this stuff on a cop's salary. Sure you weren't taking a little something under the table? Skimming a drug bust or two to keep yourself in … Waterford?" Kate burst out laughing.

"What's so funny?"

"Nothing, Coop. I think I'm just tired, and you kind of surprise me." Kate stepped closer to inspect the sparkling and, she noted, dust-free collection. "Where'd you get this?" She ran her hand down an exquisitely cut vase on the top shelf.

"You have a very good eye, Kate. That's the most valuable piece I've got. And my favorite. It was a gift from an old girlfriend. An attorney."

"I'm impressed."

"That I dated an attorney or that she spent a lot of money on me?"

"Honestly? Both."

"Gee, thanks." Cooper turned and walked across the living room. "Give me a minute. I need to check and see what I've got available for dinner. Didn't know I'd be having company." He stopped and grinned at Kate. "Can I get you a beverage? I do have a nice chardonnay already chilled."

Kate couldn't help herself. She burst out laughing. "That would be lovely."

"Oh, I get it." Cooper made a show of scratching his belly. "How's about a can a Bud, baby? Feel better now?"

"Wine would be delightful."

While Cooper busied himself with the food, Kate took the opportunity to make a closer inspection of the interior of his home. The structure was originally built around the turn of the century, an adobe construction that had grown and changed over the years. A stunning stone fireplace, built from blue-green copper-bearing minerals like chrysocolla and malachite, filled one corner from floor to ceiling. The walls, bricks of sun-dried earth and straw, were covered with Native American weavings. A few pieces of what looked like very old pottery were interspersed with obviously contemporary creations that Kate could see were picked for their complimentary colors and odd shapes. A brightly colored rug lay across the ruddy Mexican tile floor. A collection of turn-of-the-century, sepia-tone photographs depicting pioneer life and set in un-matching frames hung above an oak credenza. The spacious couch, filled with hand woven, southwestern-design pillows, faced the fireplace. Resting in front of the couch was a glass-top coffee table constructed from an ornamental wrought iron gate.

Kate sank into the couch, marveling at the effort it must have taken to choose and place each object so perfectly in the room. She thought of the mess in her house.

A scratching sound distracted her. Then a thump.

Kate scanned the room. Another thump drew her to a back wall and a dog door. The flap pushed open, revealing the head and front legs of the biggest desert tortoise she'd ever seen.

"Cooper!" She jumped from the comfort of the couch.

"What?" He entered the room holding a tray with a plate of warm Brie, a small baguette, and a spray of purple grapes. Cooper followed Kate's gaze and watched the animal plop over the three-inch lip onto the floor.

Kate, eyebrows raised, looked at her host.

"His name is Ralph." Cooper placed the tray on the coffee table.

"You have a pet ... tortoise?"

"Ralph is not my pet." Cooper sliced the bread and slathered on some warm cheese. He handed the appetizer to Kate. "Hold on. I'll be right back with the wine."

"What do you mean he's not your pet?" Kate watched the animal trudge across the floor. She noticed the tortoise was missing a hind leg.

"He just lives here." Cooper called from the kitchen. "He is free to come and go in the yard. I found him hit by a car out on Route 8. I took him to the vet and they amputated his leg. I kept him confined until he healed. He can't be released back into the wild, so we are room-mates."

"And you put in a dog door for a turtle?" Kate grinned.

"Of course not." Cooper returned with two white wine glasses and an ice bucket that was holding an open bottle of chardonnay. "Do you think I'm a boob? The cat door is for the cat."

"You also have a cat?"

"Why would I have a cat door and not a cat?"

"Because they don't sell turtle doors?" Kate offered as he poured the wine.

"Wiseass. I happen to have a calico cat who is probably at this very moment harassing some poor gecko and biting off its legs one at a time so she can play with it while it spins round and round. Or maybe she's sleeping."

"I heard they're pretty good at that." Kate sipped her wine enjoying the fruity tang of apples and pears.

"It is what they do best. Cats sleep about eighteen hours a day. That's why I intend to come back as somebody's pampered puss. I'm sure you'll meet Martha later when she feels the time is right."

Cooper clinked his wine glass to hers. "You know you're supposed to wait for the toast, Butler. What are you, a barbarian?"

The tortoise, which had now crossed the floor, stood poised with both front legs on Cooper's foot, head straining upward.

"I'm no turtle expert, but I think he's begging," Kate said.

"Tortoise, Kate, not a turtle." Cooper handed Ralph a grape, which the animal took in its mouth. "That's all you get, Ralphie. So make it last."

"Who the hell are you?" Kate didn't know Cooper at all.

"Too much fruit in his diet isn't good for him," he answered, ignoring her question. "I'll miss Ralph."

"Where's he going?"

"He'll be in hibernation over the winter. He has a burrow out back under the creosote bushes by the rocks. I won't see him again until spring."

"I'm sorry for your loss." Kate said with mock sincerity.

38

KATE, SHOWERED AND DRESSED, was glad she always had the foresight to keep extra clothes in the truck. When she was still in TV, Kate was never sure where she might be at the end of the day, but now that packed bag wedged behind the front seat was simply a habit she couldn't seem to break.

Kate paced Cooper's living room, anxious to find answers to both the sabotage of the Sunset Limited and the kidnapping of Kelly Garcia. She checked her watch and resisted calling the deputy again. Since she was a notoriously restless sleeper, Kate couldn't believe she'd conked out on his couch for ten hours. Of course, there were the two bottles of wine and the snifter of Bailey's to consider.

She stopped in front of a photograph in an ornate silver frame. Cooper, wet hair slicked back, and a dark-haired beauty in a honey-colored sarong. Smiling in some tropical setting, they both seemed horribly happy.

Kate remembered dinner and had to admit the cop put on quite a show. The stuffed pork chops had been thick and juicy, flavored with sprigs of rosemary grown in his backyard herb garden. Small red and purple potatoes were basted in olive oil, rolled in sea salt and cracked black pepper, skewered, and roasted whole on the grill. String beans, sautéed with thinly sliced onions and Portobello mushrooms, were served in a delicate, green and white, shamrock-covered bowl. Kate knew the pattern, recognized it was Belleek china made in Ireland. Dessert consisted of brownies topped with Ben & Jerry's Heath Bar Crunch ice cream and came with an apology that he didn't have time to make something more worthy of her visit. Next time, he'd do bananas Foster, he'd said.

Next time? All the years she and Cooper had been acquainted and she knew so little about him.

Kate pushed open the back door and walked into the midmorning sun. She slumped into a royal blue wrought iron butterfly chair. Sipping the strong black coffee Cooper brewed before heading into the office, she listened to the cacophony of desert noises swirling around her, sounds made all the more vivid because there was no competition from electronic noise, sounds that would have been muted at Kate's house by the TV that was always on. She had not seen a television anywhere in Cooper's home.

Birds warbled and chirped and whistled around her, going about their daily work. A red-tailed hawk circled, searching for a meal. A huge black insect droned by and would have sent Kate running for cover had she not recognized the giant as a carpenter bee. The harmless creature sounded like a miniscule helicopter.

Turning her attention to the sheets of paper she'd retrieved from Cooper's fax machine, Kate perused the information. The text of the letter found at the wreck scene continued to baffle her, as it did the local and federal authorities whose specialists were studying the writing and content for clues. Klanwatch, a group that kept tabs on domestic terrorists, had no files pertaining to a militia named Sons of Gestapo. The letter was aimed at law-enforcement agencies including the Federal Bureau of Alcohol, Tobacco and Firearms, the FBI, the state police, and even the county sheriff. Also mentioned were the government sieges at Ruby Ridge and Waco. Kate thought the hodgepodge of information was strange, scattered. Domestic terrorists were usually more specific in their agenda.

A Mexican bird-of-paradise shuddered at the edge of the flagstone patio. The plant's ball-shaped orange blooms rustled as Ralph emerged and plodded her way.

The front door slammed, and Kate hollered "I'm out back." She watched the tortoise. He reached her foot, his head strained upward, no doubt in search of a grape or some other tortoise-type treat.

"Good morning." Cooper graced Kate with a bright smile.

"That was quick."

"Not much is happening." His eyes shifted to the tortoise. "Jesus, Ralph. Why do you always have to hit on my women?"

Kate raised her eyebrows.

"Just a figure of speech." He bent down, and took hold of the animal. Cooper lifted the turtle up to eye level. "Cool it, Ralph. Begging does not become you." The tortoise's head bobbed and weaved.

"You're goofy." Kate finished the last of her coffee.

The phone rang. "Excuse me." Cooper placed the tortoise gently under a nearby creosote bush and walked back into the house. When he returned, he had a serious look on his face. "Pat Sanders called. He wants to talk. Let's drive out there."

"Great!" Kate jumped from her seat in the butterfly chair. "I was starting to get a little stir-crazy."

"Life in the outback is a bit too tame for a big city girl?"

"No, it's not that. It's just that I'm so used to having to be somewhere all the time. In the news business, you're always scrambling to get to where the story is. You're always playing catch-up. I've been living like that a long time."

"I understand," Cooper said. "Police work is pretty much the same way."

39

COOPER GUIDED THE BLAZER off of Hyder Road
and into what had become the parking lot for the federal
and state workers who'd been assigned to the wreck site.

"By the way, they've got that student in Tucson sitting
with a sketch artist." He shut down the engine. "A drawing
should give us a better idea of who we're looking for.
Hopefully, we'll be able to get a copy by noon."

"What about the other passengers who saw him?" Kate
asked.

"The kid got the best look at him. He said they worked
together about ten minutes getting the girl out of the car.
He's a college boy. They say he seems pretty astute. Maybe
we'll get lucky and get a good likeness."

The Blazer doors opened and slammed in unison, and
Kate and Cooper walked to the FBI tent for a meeting
with Pat Sanders.

A short time later, the FBI chief handed a magazine to
Cooper. The periodical, titled *SP Trainline*, was the most
recent issue. "We need to take a look at anyone locally with
a connection to the railroad. Open it. Take a look at the
article I've marked."

Cooper flipped to a page tagged with a bright yellow Sticky. Kate stood close to him so she could also read the text. It took a couple of minutes for the significance of the article to sink in.

"Jesus!" Cooper closed the magazine. "It's all here. This is a copycat-crime right down to the wiring. This article should be titled 'Train Sabotage for Dummies.'"

"All they had to do was follow the instructions," Kate said. "There's even a diagram."

Sanders nodded. "Though they did need to have the right equipment. Still, it's scary. The poor guy that wrote the story, what's his name again?"

Cooper checked the article again. "John Signor,"

"Yeah, Signor. Here he's getting paid to write a nice little historical piece about a derailment fifty-six years ago in Harney, Nevada, and some yahoo decides to recreate the crime."

"Says here twenty-four people died in that crash, and that the saboteurs were never caught." Cooper handed the magazine to Kate.

"The bad news is not much has changed in regard to the way trains function in the last fifty-six years." Sanders sat and motioned to Cooper and Kate to join him. "So, what worked back then, works just as well today."

"I've never seen this magazine before." Kate flipped to the cover of the periodical. "What kind of subscription rate does it have?"

"We're lucky in that department. It's got a very small circulation compared to most magazines. Only about twelve hundred people are on the mailing list. Mostly hobbyists. It caters to railroad buffs. The magazine's devoted entirely to Southern Pacific Railroad history, and it only comes out four times a year."

"That means our saboteurs decided to do this pretty spur of the moment," Cooper said. "This is the most recent issue?"

"Correct."

"How many subscribers live in Arizona?" Kate asked.

Sanders reached into a stack of papers on the table and found the one he wanted. "Fourteen. I was hoping maybe one of the names might ring a bell. We're prepared to check each one, but since you're familiar with the locals, I thought I'd run the list by you first." He handed the page to Cooper.

"The only one I recognize is Carl James." He gave the list back to the FBI man. "But I don't think he'll help you. He's been dead maybe six months. Liver cancer."

"Is there any way to find out if the magazine was delivered to him?" Kate asked.

"Unless someone cancels subscriptions, they generally just keep coming as long as they've been paid for."

"I know James's son," Cooper said. "He's not the most easy-going guy. Ex con. Why not let me check into it?"

40

"HEY, RAMM," the proprietor of the Butterfield General Store called from his usual spot behind the counter. Various publications were spread before him, all with lead articles concerning the wreck of the Sunset Limited. "Can you believe this?" He observed as Ramm grabbed a cardboard carton.

"Do they have any idea who might have done it?" Ramm inquired casually.

Tom Pace slipped his glasses from his forehead and adjusted them so he could read. "Says right here in the *Arizona Republic* that they're still goin' over the crime scene. Only one person died."

Ramm looked over. By some fortuitous stroke of luck had the deceased been Miranda? His hopes were dashed when Tom continued his oratory.

"Just that poor railroad worker. I guess he was up doin' his rounds while most everyone else was sleepin'. They're sayin' that's what saved 'em. 'Bout one hundred were injured, but most of 'em weren't hurt bad."

"Pretty lucky." Ramm worked his way down the shelves.

"No word on Kelly. Funny, there's nothin' in the papers

or on the TV 'bout her missin'. Now who would wanna go and take that poor little thing?"

He didn't give Ramm time to respond.

"And that letter. Damn odd if you ask me. Started out with some poem about women prayin' at that Branch Davidian compound over in Waco. Prayin' by the light of kerosene lamps right after the electricity was cut off. Guess whoever wrote it didn't like the way the government treated Koresh and his group."

At the mention of the Branch Davidian leader, Ramm froze. *Madman or Messiah?* It made no difference in the end. David Koresh died along with his believers in what turned into a public relations disaster for the Federal Government. Could Dr. Bar El have prevented the annihilation had Koresh been treated at Kfar Shaul? Would he have become just another tourist stricken by the ancient city's mysteries, only to return home chastened and embarrassed by the experience?

"Ramm! Hey, Ramm! You alright?" Tom stood at his side, griping him by the shoulder.

"Sure, I'm fine," Ramm shook his head. The storeowner seemed unconvinced. Both men stooped to pick up the cans of tuna Ramm had no memory of knocking to the floor. "I'm sorry, Tom. I must still have a touch of flu."

"You aren't lookin' too good, if you ask me."

The groceries were boxed and paid for. Tom helped Ramm carry them to the truck. "Got rid of that dog, did ya?" He squinted at the empty front seat in the cab.

"No, just left her home today. Don't worry, I'm keeping her." Ramm forced a smile. "Oh, shit! I forgot I need a quart of ice cream. Mint chocolate chip, if you have any."

Tom stared at Ramm, fingering a pen he kept in his shirt pocket.

"Do you have any?" Ramm asked again.

"I think I've got one left. Let me check."

The proprietor returned a few minutes later holding a brown paper bag. "Here you go. Double wrapped it, but you better get it home pretty quick."

"Thanks." Ramm peeled off a five to pay for the ice cream.

"It's on me," Tom waved the money away. "Though I don't recollect you ever havin' much of a taste for ice cream."

Twenty minutes later, the bell in the store rang. "Elect Sun." Tom peered over his glasses. "How about that wreck?"

"Such a horrible thing. I don't know how people can commit such violence."

"Any word on Kelly?"

"Not yet. I was hoping you might have heard something."

Tom looked at the woman. "Not a word. In fact, I ain't even seen her mentioned in the papers."

"They're not releasing any information until the authorities determine exactly what's happened."

"And the reason for that?"

"I'm not sure, but they must deal with this kind of thing frequently. I'm sure they know what's best." Elect Sun placed her few purchases on the counter. "But Kelly must be located. The baby is due soon."

"When you think about it, there are only two possibilities." Tom dropped his glasses to the counter. "Either the people who derailed the train found some reason to take Kelly, which probably wouldn't be good. Or she is with someone who is tryin' to protect her."

Elect Sun nodded. "You mean someone *rescued* her from the train? A friend?"

"Maybe so."

"But why not come forward?" she asked. "Bring her back, now that she's out of danger?"

Tom looked directly at the woman. "I don't know, but I think someone is tryin' to help her."

"Maybe." Elect Sun turned toward the door.

"By the way, Ramm was in just before you got here. He bought hisself a quart of mint chocolate chip ice cream."

41

"HEY, BUCK!" Cooper called, as he and Kate stepped inside the tiny front office of the Dateland Gas Station.

"Deputy." Buck James entered through the rear door. "I was out back working on my transmission. What's up?" The brutish man stopped and suggestively eyed Kate.

"This is Kate Butler."

"You livin' here abouts, honey?" Buck proffered a lecherous grin.

"No, just visiting." Kate stared down the thick-armed mechanic whose vein-stained nose pegged him as a heavy drinker. Spiderweb tattoos on his elbows marked him as an ex-con.

"You know about the train wreck, Buck?"

"Sure." He wiped the wrench he was holding with a greasy rag.

"I was wondering whether you've gotten any magazines in the mail lately. One's that might be addressed to Carl?"

"Hell! He's been dead over six months now. Why would ya care what he might be gettin' in the mail?"

"We're looking for a magazine called *SP Trainline*," Kate said.

"Are ya? You a cop, honey?"

"She's just a friend." Cooper shot a glance at Kate. "Still, we'd like to see the magazine if you have it."

"Guess I shouldn't have been considerin' this a social call. I don't talk to no cops without an attorney present." Buck turned. "I got work to do on my transmission."

"Gosh, Buck." Kate walked toward him, smiling sweetly. "This doesn't have anything to do with you. We're just trying to locate a copy of a magazine that might have been sent to your father. Nobody's talking about a crime. His name's on a list of people who've received it, and we'd like to take a look at it."

Buck coldly appraised her, making no effort to mask his gaze as he inched his way over her body. "Honey, you must think I'm just some stupid country boy. But today's your lucky day, 'cause I ain't done nothin' wrong. So yea, my daddy got the magazine. Been gettin' it for years."

"You still have it? The one that came this month?"

Buck thought for a moment. "Don't remember seein' it. Then again, didn't see much mail over the last week."

"Why is that?" Cooper asked.

"Don't know. I asked the mailman. Said he delivered a wad a stuff. But my box was empty."

"You're saying somebody stole your mail and might have picked up the magazine in the process?"

"Maybe. Don't know. But I ain't never seen that magazine. Not in three or four months."

"You know anybody who might wanna rifle your mail?" Cooper asked.

Buck narrowed his eyes while his hands worked harder cleaning the wrench. "That boy a mine. Little half-breed prick. He's been around causin' trouble wherever he goes. Coulda grabbed the mail just to piss me off."

"Your son? I thought you told me he isn't around here much."

"Yeah, he lives with his momma in L.A."

"Is he there now?" Kate asked.

"Don't know. Don't care. Hope I never see the little bastard again." Buck turned to Cooper. "Kid robbed me. He was here a few days ago. Took my old Chevy and everything else he could get his hands on. Ain't seen him since."

"Could you give me his full name? And an address if you have one?" Cooper reached for his notepad.

"Why should I?"

"Maybe we can help you get your things back?" Kate said.

Buck appraised her again and finally said, "Okay."

42

KELLY MODELED THE turquoise pullover and matching pants. She also wore a pair of bright white Reeboks.

"Big improvement." Ramm nodded. "You like the shoes?"

"They feel better than any shoes I've ever had." She marveled at the soft cushioning provided by the thick rubber soles.

"They fit all right? Not too tight? I had to guess the size."

"They fit just fine, Jason. Thank you."

"You're certainly welcome. There are some shirts and socks in the other bag."

"Not just for the clothes." Kelly pulled her gaze away from the shoes and looked at Ramm. "Not many people have been nice to me. Most, when they see me, turn their heads and act like I'm not even there. Or they speak to me like I'm a child who doesn't understand. Thank you for talking to me without looking away. Thank you for being my ... friend."

"You just haven't known that many people yet." He smiled as brightly as he could. "You'll have lots of friends someday."

"Do you really think so?" Kelly twirled in her new shoes.

"Yes, I do. Now let's get some lunch, because I have something special for dessert."

"Ice cream?"

"You'll see. And then, I'm going down to talk to Elect Sun to tell her you're here," he said mostly to convince himself that he would. "We'll figure out the best place for you to live. Okay?"

"Okay."

"Let's eat."

Ramm and Kelly prepared dinner.

"What are my choices?" she asked as Ramm pulled three packages of pasta out of the cupboard.

"Let's see. We've got angel hair, bow ties and, my personal favorite, the squiggly screw-up kind that stick on your fork."

Kelly giggled.

"You choose." He opened another cabinet door and checked the shelves. "Oops! No sauce. But don't worry. I've got a case out in the shed. Give me a minute. I'll be right back."

Ramm started for the door, then stopped and turned around. "Why don't you go around back by the tack barn? Pick some basil. You know what that looks like?"

"Elect Sun taught me about herbs. I'll go get some." Kelly walked out of the kitchen, letting the screen door swing shut behind her.

The air was cool; a hint that autumn had finally arrived in the desert. Ramm opened the door to the small, thick-walled block building he'd put up to house extra supplies. Since there were no windows, it was dark inside, which kept the building cooler during the hot months. Ramm reached for the switch on the wall. He was greeted by a brief flash, a loud pop, and then darkness. Ghostly images floated through the darkened room.

"Shit!" Ramm remembered he was out of light bulbs. He could unscrew one in the living room and replace the broken bulb, but he had a good idea where the tomato sauce was and trusted himself in the murky darkness. Ramm opened the door wide, to let in some light, and worked his way to the back of the shed, grateful he always kept the place neat. He couldn't remember exactly which shelf the jars were on, but he did recall the tomato sauce containers had a raised design on the glass and metal screw lids covering large openings on the top. Ramm moved his hands over the stock of supplies searching for the right jar.

On the second shelf, he felt the pain. Pulling his injured wrist away violently, he knocked over a number of jars, sending them crashing to the floor. Glass and liquid foodstuff splattered on the concrete.

Ramm focused on the pain in his wrist. Taking several deep breaths, he willed himself to be calm, and walked slowly out of the darkened shed. He crossed the backyard to the kitchen steps, holding his arm up before him.

"Kelly!" he tried to keep the panic out of his voice so as not to frighten the girl. He pushed the door open with his foot. *Why did a simple insect bite have him so disturbed?*

She sat at the table cleaning a bunch of fresh basil, separating the deep-green leaves from the stalks. "What's wrong? What's all over your pants? Is that blood?"

"No. No, just sauce, I think. It was dark, and I knocked some jars over. Something bit me." Ramm grimaced, a wave of pain caused by a contraction in his injured hand. "Go out to the truck, Kelly. There's a first aid kit behind the front seat."

Ramm moved into the living room and sat on the edge of the couch. A few minutes later, the medical supply box lay open before him on the coffee table. He surveyed the bite, which appeared to be the work of a spider of some kind, though he was unable to discern the variety from the tiny punctures. A black widow was a possibility, but the spider's poison would not spread so quickly, and this felt different from bites black widows had inflicted on him in the past. A scorpion, maybe—he'd seen many around the cabin—but he knew their sting usually caused a severe burning sensation.

Ramm dismissed both creatures. That left him with the possibility that the bite had been the work of a brown recluse, a spider whose venom usually took several hours to work into the victim's system. Ramm noted the location of the wound. The animal's bite lay on top of one of the large veins on the inner side of his wrist. He reasoned that might be why the poison seemed to be moving through him so quickly.

Ramm wracked his brain for other poisonous Sonoran Desert creatures that might have been lurking on the dark shelves in the shed, but suddenly found concentration difficult. A crippling wave of nausea struck him. He began to shiver violently.

"Kelly!" Ramm lay down on the couch. "Cover me with a blanket. Keep me warm so I don't go into shock. Clean the bite with antiseptic."

He retched. Nothing came up.

Kelly frantically searched through the packets and bottles in the first aid kit, dug under bandages, tubes of creams and gels, scissors, tweezers, needles, eyewash.

"Which one, Jason? Which one is antiseptic? I can't *read.*"

But Ramm didn't answer. He'd passed out.

43

COOPER SAT AT THE DESK in his home office and read through the notes he'd taken on the disappearance of Kelly Garcia.

Kate snooped through the contents of the bookshelf that covered an entire wall. "Now I know what you do in your spare time." She eyed the titles. "*Dante's Inferno, Baseball's Greatest Quotes, John Toland's Adolf Hitler: Volumes 1 and 2, Sacajawea,* and *Rodale's Illustrated Encyclopedia of Herbs.* You're one eclectic son-of-a-bitch, Coop."

"Admit it. You find me fascinating." He winked at Kate and picked up a new document from the fax machine.

"What are you reading?"

"William Carl James. Eighteen years old. Resides at 2534 North Rachel Road in Los Angeles. Son of Buck James and Karina Lopez. Our boy's got priors for disorderly conduct, assault, shoplifting, and animal mutilation."

"How nice." Kate grimaced.

"He's also got a sealed juvy record, so our boy's been busy."

"Buck said he's been out here a couple of weeks. What did he come back for?"

"Good question. Especially when you consider the kid probably wasn't here to visit dear old dad. Take a look at this." Cooper handed Kate a case file from the Child Protective Services.

She scanned the printout. "Six home visits. The boy was beaten. Burned with cigarettes. Suffered a broken arm and nose, and multiple lacerations requiring twenty stitches. That last one put Buck in prison for eighteen months." She stared at Cooper. "That's all he got? Eighteen months? That's disgusting. How's that possible?"

"Maybe he pled out."

Kate looked at the accompanying pictures of the dark-haired boy with the steely dead eyes and high cheekbones, the front and side views above the numbers marking Billy's permanent place in California's penal system.

"Though I hate to admit it, there's a part of me that wants to feel sorry for the kid," she said. "What were his chances in life with a father like Buck?"

"We all make choices, Kate. There are plenty of people with horrendous backgrounds who have gone on to make something of themselves."

"You think it's all about choice, Coop? We are totally in control of who we are and what we become?"

"Not completely. I do believe some people are just born evil. Their wiring is off. Someday, when scientists have cut into enough bad-guy brains, they'll discover something is out of whack. That's why I'm completely against conjugal visits for the real miscreants. Though I'm sure the American Civil Liberties folks would disagree, I don't think we need to be spreading those serial criminal genes out into the population."

Kate leaned up against the edge of the desk. "From what I've read, there are plenty of women willing to marry and multiply with the Charles Mansons of the world."

Cooper shook his head. "You're a woman. Help me with that. How can anyone be drawn to monsters like Ted Bundy and John Wayne Gacy?"

"It's called low self-esteem. Make that no self-esteem," Kate picked up a document from the edge of Cooper's desk. "Still, the girl always knows where her man is when he's behind bars."

"I guess that's a plus." Cooper paused.

"What?"

"I just remembered something. Elect Peter said Kelly was accosted by some guy nobody recognized?"

"That's right."

"Wanna bet our boy Billy was looking for a little 'strange' and came across the girl? Maybe it wasn't the first time. Maybe he'd seen her before."

"Maybe he's got her hidden away somewhere." Kate shivered at the thought.

Cooper grabbed the phone, punched in the numbers, and waited for the captain to pick up. "Buddy."

"Cooper."

"Put out an APB on a Chevy Cavalier. Baby blue. Arizona license plate number 865GPE."

Kate tapped Cooper on the shoulder and pointed to the document she held. She ran her finger halfway down the page, stopping at what she wanted the deputy to see.

He read the list of weapons Buck James claimed were missing from his trailer. "And Buddy, the driver, Billy James, is dangerous and may be armed."

"Noted," Buddy said. "Also, Elect Sun wants you to call her. She says it's very important."

"Did she say what it's about?"

"No, she didn't have your number and just asked that you call her as soon as you have a chance."

44

ELECT SUN, EXHAUSTED from weeding the vegetable garden, knelt in the soft dark earth between small heirloom tomato plants and a row of sweet corn. The crunch of a vehicle on gravel drew her attention to the front drive where she saw Deputy Cooper's Blazer pull to a stop. Her heart pounded. Had Kelly been located and, if so, what condition was she in? She rose to meet the deputy.

"Elect Sun." Cooper strode across the yard.

He was smiling. Surely, it was good news.

Elect Sun relaxed a little.

The kitchen door slammed. Elect Peter walked through the shade of the giant cottonwood to join them. "Any word?"

"No, not yet. I'm sorry. I don't have anything good to tell you. We're still looking for Kelly, but we do have some information about a man who was seen at the wreck site."

Elect Peter motioned Cooper and Kate to some white plastic chairs under the tree. He and Elect Sun sat on the slatted cedar swing. They listened as the deputy explained how the University of Arizona student helped retrieve the unconscious girl from the wreckage, and how the man carried Kelly off into the darkness.

"Tell me what this man looked like." Elect Peter focused on Cooper.

"Caucasian, six two or so, pale eyes, slender, muscular. We should have a sketch later today. We'll get a copy over to you as soon as we get it. Sound like anyone you know?"

Neither Elect Sun nor Elect Peter spoke.

"I ... don't know." Elect Sun avoided eye contact with the deputy.

"How about someone who resembles this man who also knows Kelly?" Kate asked. "You've both said she was acquainted with very few people."

"That's true." Elect Sun pressed her hands together and held them in her lap.

Cooper watched the woman stare at the ground. "Elect Sun, the girl is pregnant. The guy might be hurting her."

"Oh, no!" Elect Sun blinked, stared at Cooper, and then looked away. "I can't imagine that. Not at all."

Cooper furrowed his brow, then stood, and checked his watch. "We're going to the office to pick up a copy of the sketch. I was assured it would be available by 4:00 p.m. I hope when we return, you'll be ready to tell us what you know."

Elect Peter nodded. Elect Sun would not meet the deputy's gaze.

The Blazer roared down the drive.

"What the hell is going on here?" Kate watched the compound's date palms race by. "It's pretty friggin' obvious they know where the girl is. They're not very adept in the lying department."

"They probably haven't had much practice." Cooper turned onto the blacktop that would lead them to Route 8.

"I suppose the good news is they seem pretty certain the girl's not in any danger." Kate noticed Cooper's tight grip on the steering wheel, and the anger etched on his face.

"They don't know anything!" He spit the words. "I can't tell you how many times I've seen people try to protect some perp, thinking he'd never harm a soul. But *I* have to sort through the body parts."

"I'm sure …"

"Trust me. You can't be sure of anything. These are naïve, cloistered people. They have no idea what goes on in the real world. You wanna know why I left Phoenix, Kate?" Cooper mashed his foot on the accelerator. "I couldn't stand the ignorance anymore. Every time some pig did something horrible, and we actually managed to catch him, all his friends and relatives came out of the woodwork, spewing sound bites to the media about what a *great* guy he was, and how they knew he couldn't possibly have knifed and burned his family. How the cops must have planted the evidence. Or my favorite, 'If only Johnny hadn't gotten in with the wrong crowd.' How come nobody's kid is ever the ringleader of the wrong crowd, Kate? Tell me that, would you?"

Cooper took the on-ramp almost skidding into the guardrail.

"Slow down, Coop. We're gonna find her."

45

KELLY SAT IN THE OVERSTUFFED chair by the fireplace and watched Ramm thrash in his sleep. He was sweating profusely. He kicked the blanket to the floor and she was startled by the sight of his arm. Puffy flesh surrounded the bite, and a bright red vein marched past his elbow and up his inner arm.

She drew a deep breath. Her legs ached, the baby was kicking, she had indigestion, and her head hurt, but she eased herself off the chair, walked to the couch, and tucked the quilt back in around Ramm.

She never saw his fist coming. It was a glancing blow to the right side of her jaw, but she was knocked off balance and fell to the floor. A hot, salty taste filled her mouth. Blood. She put a finger to her lip and it came away red. Small droplets landed on the carpet. Kelly dabbed the wound with the hem of her sweatshirt. She opened and shut her mouth several times checking the damage. She'd be bruised, but if Ramm had hit her squarely, she could have easily been knocked out.

Kelly eyed the sleeping man. He was mumbling something incoherent in his sleep. She struggled to her feet and backed away. She looked down at Dog. "I have to go get help." She patted the animal on the head. It was the right decision. "Jason said there's no phone here, so I'll go find Elect Peter. He'll take care of Jason's arm."

But finding the way to the compound of the Children of Light would not be easy. Kelly wasn't exactly sure where Ramm's cabin was situated. While she could tell directions from the position of the sun, she didn't know which way to go. She hadn't seen any homes or other people on their walks, though she had noticed bright green, cultivated fields in the distance where there must certainly be a farmhouse and people.

The keys to Ramm's truck lay on the mantel above the fireplace. Kelly fingered the Green Beret emblem on the chain. She had never driven before.

Ramm moaned again. His teeth were chattering now. She had no choice. She grabbed two blankets from the bed and carefully spread them over and around him, constantly wary of his hands. When she was satisfied he was warm enough, she collected the keys and headed for the yard.

Kelly sat in the driver's seat of Ramm's black truck, blood oozing from her broken lip. She checked her face in the rearview mirror and wiped the blood with the back of her hand.

She tried the keys on the ring until one slipped into the slot on the steering column. She turned the key and the engine switched on. Gripping the wheel with both hands, she studied the dashboard. What should she do next? Kelly closed her eyes and envisioned sitting in the truck next to Eduardo. She reached for the gearshift, but couldn't force the handle to move. She saw the markings P R N D 2 1, but didn't know what they meant.

Inadvertently, Kelly pulled the gearshift toward her, slipping the transmission into reverse. The truck lurched backward. Even if the seat hadn't been adjusted for a man of Ramm's height, Kelly wouldn't have known to put her foot on the brake. The truck traveled backward down the drive and picked up speed as it descended down the hill. Kelly tried to steer, causing the vehicle to career wildly from side to side.

Turning to look behind her, she saw the hard turn in the road, a bend made to skirt a massive pile of tailings left from the days when the Rowley was a working mine. Kelly tried to force the door to the cab open, but before she could, the truck plunged off the road down into a shrub-filled ditch and slammed into the base of the rock pile. When the pickup's rear end made contact with the boulders, Kelly felt a hard jolt.

She placed her hand on her belly and said a grateful prayer that she had remembered to put the seat belt on. She shut down the engine, opened the door, and got out to survey the damage. The right rear tire was flat, the bumper and passenger side panel caved in.

Kelly walked slowly up the road back to the cabin wishing she wasn't pregnant. Usually quick and agile, she could have run for help, but that possibility was out of the question.

As she approached the yard, Kelly heard Becky whinny from the corral. After making her way around back, Kelly stared at the Appaloosa. She'd ridden a few times with her father, but certainly not eight months pregnant. Kelly watched the horse paw the ground, then gallop off to the other side of the enclosure. Suddenly, the animal seemed very large.

A short time later, Kelly stared at the equipment she'd gathered. Unable to figure out how to secure the saddle and bridle, she discarded both for a rope halter and a thick black and brown Navajo saddle blanket. She looped the rope she found in the tack shed over the horse's head, and led the animal to the side of the corral. Kelly tied the line tightly to a post, then climbed the fence, speaking gently to the horse as she moved. She progressed slowly. Finally, Kelly eased one leg, then the other, up over the top rail, but when she reached for Becky, the horse shied away.

"Easy, girl," Kelly grasped the Appaloosa's mane. After coaxing the animal toward her, she awkwardly pulled herself onto the horse's back. At that moment, Kelly froze. She had neglected to pack any food or water, but she might not be able to remount the horse and Ramm was suffering. She had to go now.

Kelly urged the animal forward.

46

THE FADED, DECADES-OLD station wagon crawled to a stop when the cabin came into view, a trail of dust floating cloud-like, marking the path the vehicle had taken up the mountain.

"Is this it?" Elect Sun searched the area, hoping for a familiar face.

"We followed Tom's directions. That spot we passed down the hill has to be the Rowley Mine. And I don't see any other inhabitable buildings around." Elect Peter slipped the handwritten map into the passenger-side visor. "Let's go."

Elect Sun gave the old beater some gas.

The only answer to their knock was a scratching sound at the door. She tried again, and this time the dog barked. "Jason," Elect Sun called out. "Jason, are you here?"

She reached for the door handle, turned the knob, and pushed the door open.

Jason Ramm, completely naked, stood staring out the picture window at the valley and the mountains beyond. He did not turn or acknowledge them.

"Oh!" Elect Sun turned away.

Elect Peter moved toward the window. "Jason, are you all right?"

When he received no answer, the doctor placed one hand on Ramm's shoulder and walked around to face him. "Let me help you, son." He took Ramm by the arm.

Ramm flinched away from his touch, and grasped the damaged arm to his chest. Elect Peter gently took hold of Ramm's hand.

"Don't you know who I am?" Ramm said.

The doctor ignored the question and led him over to the couch.

"Please sit down, Jason. Let me take a look at your arm."

Elect Peter had momentarily forgotten about Elect Sun. Now, he saw the shock on her face. The doctor guided Ramm to the couch and covered his lap with a blanket.

"Elect Sun, see if you can find a robe or some pajamas for Jason." He nodded toward what appeared to be the bedroom door.

Elect Sun, who had been frozen in her spot, blinked and quickly left the room.

The doctor turned his attention back to Ramm. He switched on a lamp to examine the wound. "It's a spider bite. Did you see what kind of spider bit you, Jason?"

No answer.

Elect Sun returned and handed over the white terrycloth robe she'd found.

"I'll need to clean Jason's arm. Could you get some warm water and towels?"

Elect Sun left the room again without a word.

His eyes searched the coffee table where the contents of the first aid kit were scattered.

After Elect Sun placed a bowl of water, a bar of soap, and a towel between the two men, she watched Elect Peter bathe the wound. "Shouldn't we get Jason to a hospital?"

"Don't you know who I am?" Ramm gazed at the woman.

Elect Sun stared into his eyes. Her hand flew to her chest, the breath caught in her throat.

Elect Peter observed the exchange. "Elect Sun, look at me." Her eyes remained fixed on Ramm.

"Sun!"

Grudgingly, she turned to the doctor.

"Let's do what we can for him here. I'm fairly certain he's not in any immediate danger. I'm sure he's uncomfortable, but a spider bite is rarely lethal."

"You *must* know me," Ramm beseeched her.

Elect Sun witnessed such total despair in his eyes she was unable to move.

"Why don't you see if there's any tea in the kitchen?" The doctor examined the wound. "Make a pot. It will do us all some good."

Elect Sun backed away slowly, but stopped abruptly by the bedroom door.

"What is it?" Elect Peter ripped open an alcohol-soaked pad and applied it to the bite.

Elect Sun disappeared, returning moments later with a shoebox marked Reebok, Ladies 8.

"Kelly's been here." She held the shoebox out for him to see. She went back into the bedroom, and this time came out with a handful of girl's clothes. "I went straight to the closet for the robe," she explained. "I didn't see these in the chair by the bed. They still have tags on them. Why would Jason buy Kelly clothes if he intended to harm her?"

She didn't wait for an answer.

"Kelly! Kelly!" Elect Sun charged out the front door to search for the girl.

Elect Peter continued cleaning the wound. "Where is Kelly, Jason?"

"Don't you know who I am?"

Elect Peter sighed. "Let me see if I can find you something for the pain." The doctor rummaged through the medications on the table. A brown plastic bottle with a white child-protective cap caught his eye. Since the container was empty, he was about to toss it aside, but the name on the label stopped him: Haloperidol.

Ten minutes later, Elect Sun returned. "She's not here. Jason's truck isn't here either."

Ramm reached over with his undamaged arm and grabbed the empty Haloperidol container from the table. Dried blood stained his knuckles. Elect Peter stood and backed away, and for the first time noticed the smudge of blood on the carpet.

47

LATER THAT DAY, Elect Sun busied herself cleaning the shelves where the Children kept the food they preserved. She dusted jars of carrots and corn, pickled peppers, strawberry jam, and dried dates. It had been agreed that she would meet with Deputy Cooper at the compound, while Elect Peter stayed at the cabin to tend to Jason and await Kelly's return.

When Kate and Cooper arrived, she met them out in the yard. Before she had a chance to speak, the deputy handed her a photocopy of a drawing.

"Do you know him?"

Elect Sun looked at the sketch. While the drawing was far from perfect, she had no trouble recognizing the face.

"Yes. I do." She handed the paper back to Cooper. "It's Jason Ramm."

"You know where he lives?"

Elect Sun nodded. "Peter is with him now. He suffered some kind of a bite and ... isn't himself."

"What does that mean?" Kate asked.

But Cooper jumped in before Elect Sun could answer. "Does he have the girl?"

"She's up there. Somewhere. But I couldn't find her." Fat tears streaked her cheeks.

"Then how do you know she's there?" Cooper asked.

"Clothes. Jason bought her shoes and clothes. So that means he had no intention of hurting her." Elect Sun looked hopeful.

Cooper ran his hand through his hair. "Let's go. You need to take us to the house."

"Please, Deputy Cooper. Don't have him arrested. I'm sure he was only trying to help Kelly."

Kate and Cooper followed the ancient blue station wagon.

"That's right, Buddy." Cooper kept his eyes on the road as he spoke to his boss on the radio. "He's been holding her in a cabin up above the Rowley Mine. Send some backup."

"Is the guy armed?" the captain asked.

"I'm not sure, though I've been told he's been incapacitated by some kind of insect bite. I'm guessing he's pretty under the weather, so I'm not too worried. Elect Peter's up there tending to him."

"And why doesn't that make me feel better? I'll send up some support."

"Thanks."

"Why do you think he took her?" Kate asked.

"Hell if I know. Maybe he's got a thing for pregnant women." Cooper saw the uncomfortable look on Kate's face. "You know as well as I do, Media Girl, there are all kinds of sickos out there."

"Okay, but let's assume there might be another reason besides deviant sexual practices. Maybe he was trying to help her."

Elect Sun veered off Painted Damsite Road onto a barely discernable track. The path was hidden by desert foliage and a rise in the landscape, but once they traveled over the top, the narrow road became clear. Kate noticed Cooper didn't even flinch when making the turnoff.

"Been out here before, Coop?"

"Several times. Every couple of years, some rockhound gets stuck at the Rowley. We usually end up having to pull them out of the main shaft. Never fails to amaze me what those guys will do for a rock."

"I'm not sure what might persuade me to intentionally crawl down a deep dark hole in the ground," Kate said. "Cold hard cash maybe. They after gold?"

"Nope. Something called wulfenite."

"Wulfen-what?"

"Wulfenite. An old miner told me there used to be huge pieces of the stuff out here. Big transparent orange crystals. I've seen some specimens taken out of the Rowley in the Mining and Mineral Museum in Phoenix. They're really quite beautiful. No one finds pieces like that anymore. Still, collectors will put themselves in harm's way for small pieces of the stuff."

They took a sharp turn. The Rowley Mine's head frame loomed before them.

"Is that what the original miners were looking for?"

"The wulfenite crystals? No, they were looking for lead," Cooper explained. "One retired miner told me he watched over thirty tons of concentrated wulfenite go into the crusher. I told that story to some collectors I met up here on a rescue, and I swear I saw tears in their eyes."

"Kind of like my grandmother," Kate said.

"How so?"

"When she was a little girl, coal was delivered down a chute into her basement. One day she went down and discovered a huge piece that had split in two. She found a perfect fern fossil imprinted on both sides of the rock."

"Did you see it?" Cooper turned the Blazer past the Rowley Mine outbuildings.

"Nope, she said it was winter and the house was cold. She threw it into the furnace with all the other hunks of coal."

48

ELECT PETER SAT ON the front steps of the cabin and
watched as the old station wagon and the deputy sheriff's
vehicle pulled to a stop on the gravel drive.

"Has Kelly come back?" Elect Sun called from the open
window of her car.

"No, I'm afraid not." The doctor shook his head.

Cooper, Kate, and Elect Sun got out of their vehicles
and mounted the steps, but Elect Peter held his arm out to
stop them. "Please, wait."

"What? What is it? Is Jason worse?" Elect Sun asked.
She tried to push past him, but Elect Peter grasped her by
the shoulders. "Just hold on a minute. I need to explain."

"Move aside, please! I have to speak to Ramm, and
I have no time to screw around." Cooper pushed past Elect
Peter.

"Wait!" The old man surprised them with the intensity
of his demand. "Remember, deputy, I'm a doctor. I want you
to know what you'll be dealing with."

"Is he armed?" Cooper asked.

"No."

"Have you seen any weapons in the house?"

"No. None."

"Take me to him, or I'll find him myself." Cooper placed both hands on the old man's shoulders and moved him from the doorway.

Jason Ramm stood before the picture window. He wore a heavy white cotton robe. His feet were bare. A large, mixed-breed dog lay beside him.

"Are you feeling better?" Elect Sun walked toward him.

Ramm stared at the woman. He raised one hand, reached over, and touched Elect Sun gently on the cheek. "Don't you know me? You, of all people."

Kate appraised Ramm—the wet hair slicked back from an angular face, intense blue eyes, the tall, lean frame.

"Mr. Ramm, we need to know where the girl is," Cooper said brusquely.

Ramm turned around, his gaze settling on the deputy. "The girl?"

"Kelly Garcia," Kate said.

"I don't know her. But I hope she comes to know me. And all of you, as well." Ramm clasped his hands together as if in prayer. "Assuredly, I say to you, unless you are converted and become as little children, you will by no means enter the kingdom of heaven."

"Matthew 18:3," Elect Peter said without hesitation.

Elect Sun took a deep breath, then looked from Ramm to Elect Peter and back again.

Ramm walked toward Cooper with his arms held out, palms turned up. "So, you have finally come to arrest me. I have been waiting."

Cooper never hesitated. He stepped over and pushed him onto the couch. The taller man fell without resistance.

"Cut the crap, pal. We've got a sixteen-year-old pregnant girl up here somewhere, and I think you know where she is. Tell me now, because the longer you wait, the worse it's going to get for you."

"I know nothing of this girl."

"Deputy Cooper! Jason was bitten by an insect. Probably a brown recluse." Elect Peter pointed to the man's bandaged arm. "While it's rare for serious harm to come to the average person when this happens, some people are more highly affected than others."

"Okay," Cooper said. "I'll play along. Like some people can die from a single bee sting or from breathing peanut dust on an airplane. So, what?"

"My point is, Jason is obviously suffering from some kind of reaction to this bite and to—"

"What?" Cooper demanded, unable to control his growing impatience.

"His lack of medication." Elect Peter went to the coffee table and retrieved the empty vial of Haloperidol. "I found three bottles in the first aid kit and two more in the bathroom. All empty." He handed the container to the deputy.

"What is it?"

"An anti-psychotic drug."

Cooper turned the bottle. "There's no name on it. Nothing that says Ramm was given a prescription for this stuff. There isn't even a pharmacy name."

"I realize that," the doctor said.

"So, where'd he get this and why is he taking it?"

Elect Peter spread his hands.

"Your opinion then, Doctor, is that the combination of going off the drugs and the bite may have pushed him over the edge?" Kate watched Elect Sun sit on the couch beside Ramm and take his hand.

"Certainly, anyone taking this type of medication should be under the care of a physician, especially when they are contemplating going off the drugs. The bite? It might have nothing to do with his reaction at all, or it may have been a catalyst."

Ramm gently extracted his hand from Elect Sun's grip, and slipped from the couch onto his knees. Ignoring everyone in the room, he began to pray.

Elect Sun's eyes welled. "There is another explanation." Tears fell freely down her cheeks. "Did it ever occur to any of you that he might … be …"

"Might be what?" Cooper eyed the praying man.

"The Messiah." Elect Sun dropped to her knees.

49

NUNZIO MARTINEZ EDGED his way slowly down the rocky side of the wash. The incline was not steep, but Nunzio was old and not as sure footed as he once was. The ancient roan, following on a rope behind him, was nearing twenty and had been bleached almost white by the desert sun. The horse suddenly jerked back, almost wrenching the lead from his gnarled hands.

"Stop it, you ugly old caballo! What is wrong? What is it you smell? What is bothering you?"

The horse was agitated, but Nunzio's constant companion was old and often cranky. He reached into the pocket of the threadbare coat he wore regardless of the temperature and patted the half-empty bottle of cheap tequila. "At least, I have something to improve *my* mood, you old witch."

The horse fell back into step. What had disturbed her? Since he was almost blind and, as usual, quite drunk, he couldn't tell. Nunzio had been moving since dawn, and because he had no watch, he wasn't exactly sure how long he and the horse had been walking, but his feet told him this might be a good time to rest a bit. There was a dry, shady creek bed not far away that was perfect for a siesta.

Despite his failing eyesight, Nunzio knew he could find the spot. He had been traipsing all across this desert since his mining days in Ajo, the tiny southern Arizona town named for the garlic bulb and famous for the mammoth pit that, in its heyday, was the oldest continually operating copper mine in the state. But when the metal's price fell, work became hard to get in Ajo, and Nunzio's feet carried him to a farm labor camp in Hyder. The migrants were paid $2.65 an hour to work in the fields, and charged $8.00 a day for their room and board—shacks with no air conditioning or conveniences of any kind. Nunzio's peers were skid row alcoholics culled from missions in Phoenix, whose post-expenses earnings ended up mostly at the Whispering Sands Bar that stood behind their dilapidated dwellings. But in 1978, three workers dropped dead, a combination of intense heat and excessive drinking. The camp was shut down, and Nunzio had nowhere to go.

Fortune smiled on the old miner the day he found the horse. Her owner had died, and when his children came to claim the man's trailer, they simply left the little roan prancing around the corral that had been pieced together from barbed wire and saguaro bones. Nunzio led her away that day. She was his only family now.

Again the horse stopped short, sniffing and snorting as she smelled the air. Nunzio looked back at the animal and all his worldly possessions. Saddlebags, blankets and plastic bags sprouted from her back and flanks. Water bottles, wrapped together with bungee cords, dangled from her neck. A large green mesh bag he'd found at the dump contained empty aluminum cans, Nunzio's main source of tequila money. In a city, the old man might have appropriated a grocery cart to carry his property, but out in the desert, the horse was infinitely more sensible.

Nunzio cocked his head. The music drifted to him on the breeze. The horse pricked up her ears. "So, I'm not crazy then. You hear the music, too, my old friend."

When the animal began moving toward the sound, Nunzio could think of no reason not to follow. He trailed the horse out of the wash, and saw a jumble of rocks—some as big as cars—all haphazardly piled together. And the ancient saguaro was there. The giant cactus with so many limbs that was almost two-hundred-years old. Nunzio had used the towering plant as a landmark many times on his journeys. He had once found shelter from a desert storm in a small cave somewhere nearby.

The music was louder now, and Nunzio recognized the words as Spanish with a smattering of terms he didn't know. A different horse whinnied loudly. Nunzio, startled by the appearance of the Appaloosa, jumped back, slipped on the scree, and fell on his bony hands and knees. Rising slowly, he approached the other horse, reached for the rope halter, and ran his leathery hands down the animal's neck and flanks.

For a moment, he thought perhaps God had provided him with another companion. He thought of what the two animals could carry, and became dizzy with excitement. But the singing brought him back from his daydream. While the horses sniffed at one another, Nunzio edged around the boulders moving closer to the singing.

Then he stopped, unsure of the vision before him. He blinked his clouded eyes several times, but the blurry apparition remained. "Madre de Dios!" He stared into the rough rock shelter in which she sat.

Kelly, unaware of the man who watched her, had just awakened from a fitful sleep. Her idea to cut west across the desert had taken her through some rough terrain, and provided no access to help. When the day's heat settled late in the afternoon, she knew from experience to seek shelter until the cooler evening temperatures arrived. The fact that she neglected to bring any water made the need to stay cool more vital.

Kelly had guided Becky to a shady spot by the rocks, grabbed her mane, and slipped off as gracefully as she could. Exhausted, and despite the kicking baby in her womb, she had drifted off to sleep.

Now she shifted uncomfortably and leaned back against the shaded indentation in the rock, her belly bulging out over her thighs. She scanned the sky and noticed towering thunderheads in the east. The monsoon had been over for at least three weeks, but an out-of-season storm was building on the horizon. Since it was too hot to move, Kelly closed her eyes, softly hummed an old lullaby, and went back to sleep.

Nunzio squeezed himself into a crevice between two boulders. Perhaps he was about to die. He reached into his pocket, grabbed the bottle, twisted off the cap, and took a long draught of tequila.

Nunzio had not been in a church for many years, but like most Mexicans, he was raised Catholic, was taught to venerate God and Jesus and the Holy Mother Mary. His roots were in a country where the Virgin appeared frequently, sometimes in a splotch on a leak-stained wall; sometimes in the twisted shape of a cactus; sometimes baked into a tortilla. Thousands flocked to these miracles to ask the Mother of God to answer their prayers.

Still, Nunzio never knew anyone who had actually seen the Holy Mother personally. Like all Catholics, he was raised on such sightings. There was the Virgin de Guadalupe and Juan Diego's miraculous cloak. He'd been taught that children in Fatima had spoken to her many times and came to no direct harm.

But why would the Holy Virgin appear to him? Nunzio grabbed for the bottle again. When he woke, the sun had shifted, and was now low in the sky with a steady breeze pushing in from the east. He remembered his vision, so Nunzio edged up over the rocks for another look. To his astonishment, she was still there, lying in the shallow stone grotto, her face with the sad appearance he had seen so many times in religious paintings and sculptures. Who else could it be? But something about her wasn't quite right. He watched intently through his alcoholic fog and clouded vision, finally realizing what made her different from the other Madonnas he had seen. This one was still pregnant.

Tears streamed down the old man's face. He knew what he must do.

As he was about to leave, Nunzio had a thought. "Keep still." He admonished the roan as he rummaged through his belongings. "Make no noise. We don't want to wake the little mother."

He selected two plastic bottles of water, a small loaf of whole wheat bread, and an orange. Looking at the offering, he realized the Holy Mother deserved better. His mind raced as he itemized his possessions. Out of his hazy past came the tale of the Wise Men, the fanciful kings bearing gold, frankincense, and myrrh. No one ever explained to Nunzio what frankincense and myrrh were, but the old miner certainly knew all about gold. A toothless smile spread across his face.

Creeping quietly toward the sleeping girl, almost expecting her to vanish as he approached, Nunzio laid the food and water on the rocky ground beside her. On top of the loaf of bread, he placed a glittering, pitted gold nugget, three inches in diameter. Then Nunzio Martinez blessed himself for the first time in many years and hurried off.

50

Cooper hung up the phone and addressed Kate, who sat on the cabin steps beside him. "Search and Rescue's been called in. And Buddy said he'd send up some of that drug. What is it?"

"Haloperidol."

"Yeah, that stuff. If Elect Peter thinks it might help jar Jesus out of his stupor, I'm willing to give it a try."

"Notice anything odd here?" Kate nodded toward the drive in front of the cabin.

Cooper looked around and shook his head.

"There's your car and Elect Sun's station wagon, but where's Ramm's vehicle? I'm guessing he doesn't walk up and down this mountain."

They split up and searched the area for any sign of a car.

"Coop! Come here!" Kate appeared from around the backside of the cabin. She waved him over and disappeared.

"Look here." She pointed at the open gate of a corral. "Looks like Ramm is missing his car *and* his horse."

Cooper saw the hay scattered on the ground, then checked the bucket attached to the fence post. Sweet grain filled the bottom half.

Kate and Cooper returned to the cabin, where they found Ramm once again stationed by the front window, staring at the western horizon.

"Where's your car, Mr. Ramm?" Cooper asked.

"I don't own one," he answered without turning toward the officer.

"And your horse?" Kate inquired.

"Nor do I own a horse."

Kate looked at the dog lying at Ramm's feet. "How about a dog? You own a dog?"

Ramm ignored them.

The front door opened revealing a baby-faced policeman. "Buddy said I was to give this to you, Deputy Cooper."

"Thanks, Bruce." Cooper accepted the manila envelope. "Do me a favor. We're looking for Mr. Ramm's vehicle. Take a look around the area, and make sure the Search and Rescue folks know it's missing."

"Yes, sir."

"Oh, and you might find a horse wandering around somewhere, as well."

"I'll get right on it." Bruce Fielding took a long look at Ramm.

"Bruce!" Cooper lifted one eyebrow.

"Yes, sir!" The young officer nodded and left.

Cooper ripped open the envelope and read the document. "Incredible." He handed the single-page document to Kate.

"Is that it?" She perused the information again.

"Apparently."

Kate was stunned. "If this is true, Ramm hasn't existed since 1971 when he was declared Missing in Action by the Army. All this time he's never had a bank account, lived anywhere, used a credit card, or had a driver's license?" Kate looked around the well-appointed cabin. "So, who owns this place?"

Cooper studied Ramm. The deputy noted the powerful hands, the athlete's build. The man stood barefoot, motionless, the white terrycloth robe falling below his knees. Outside the window, fast moving clouds obscured the late afternoon sun.

"Even the FBI files turned up nothing." Cooper said. "Makes me think something very weird is going on here."

"You mean other than the fact he thinks he's Jesus Christ." Kate laughed.

"Is that necessary?" Elect Sun said icily as she entered the room with a tray of sandwiches.

"Um, I'm sorry, Elect Sun. I'm sarcastic out of habit. But you must admit, this is very strange," Kate nodded toward Ramm. "And we're just trying to get Kelly back."

At the mention of Kelly's name, Ramm turned and faced the others. "Kelly?" he said as if trying to recall something important. "Kelly."

The door burst open. "Found the truck," Fielding said. "It's down at the bottom of the hill. It was hidden in some brush. I'll show you."

Ten minutes later, Kate watched Cooper, hands clad in latex gloves, work his way through the vehicle. "How'd it get down here?"

"Backwards." He checked the glove box.

Kate eyed the truck's backend, which was stuck in a ditch, nose tilted up toward the road. "Your powers of deduction are impressive. No wonder you're a detective."

"And that looks like blood on the steering column."

51

WHEN KELLY FINALLY woke, she was astonished to find the sun had already set. "Oh! Stop that!" she admonished the baby kicking at her ribs.

Kelly pushed at the stone wall and tried to stand, but stopped and sat back down, amazed to see two water bottles resting before her. She reached over, grabbed one of the containers, and greedily sucked the liquid. She wiped her mouth with one hand, and reached for the bread with the other, but her hand lingered, poised over the food, when she saw the glitter. Kelly grasped the oddly-shaped object. The nugget was heavy, lumpy in places, smooth in others, and it reflected the moonlight as she turned the metal over in her hands.

Then the moon glow vanished. Kelly gazed up at the sky where fast-moving clouds hid the orb. The wind had picked up and she shivered. A storm was definitely coming.

Kelly took a few quick bites of bread and pocketed the stone. The horse, having wandered over, began sniffing at the water bottles.

"I'm sorry." Kelly rubbed the animal's nose. She stood using the horse as an anchor, then tilted the bottle, spraying a stream of water into the Appaloosa's mouth. While some of the precious fluid disappeared into the parched earth, most of the water was lapped up by the thirsty horse.

She remembered Ramm. Sick. Alone. She stroked the horse's neck and whispered, "Come on, Becky. We have to go before the rain."

Kelly reached for the other water bottle. She had no bag, so she lifted the sweatshirt up over her head, placed it on the ground, and deposited the bottle in the middle. Then, she paused. For the first time, she questioned where the provisions had come from.

"Hello!" Kelly called into the darkness. "Is anybody there?" But no answer came.

After folding the food and water tightly in the middle of the sweatshirt, Kelly wrapped the arms around her waist, tying a knot in the front. She shivered. The thin, cotton T-shirt she wore would not keep her warm for long, so she decided to ride bareback in order to keep the blanket available should she get cold. She folded the cover and draped it across the horse's neck. Now, she had to get on the beast.

The area was covered with dark boulders pocked with tiny holes, remnants of bubbles from when the rocks were molten. Slowly, she worked her way to the top of one, holding the rope tightly in an effort to keep Becky still. When she'd mounted the boulder, Kelly grasped the Appaloosa's mane.

A sharp sound, Kelly recognized instantly. She froze. The horse's eyes bulged in fear and the animal danced, reared back, and tried to get away. The rope ripped from Kelly's hand, but she kept hold on the mane and was jerked off her feet.

The snake lunged at the four-footed monster, but the horse's sharp front hooves came down hard on the coiled creature, severing the rattler's head. The jolt broke Kelly's grip, and sent her plunging onto the rocks. The horse, in terror, bolted in a wild gallop and escaped into the open desert.

"No! No! Becky, come back!" Kelly screamed, scooting away from the still wriggling body of the rattler. Though the snake was dead, the rattles still shook and the mouth still hissed while both ends waited for the message of the diamondback's demise.

She tried to stand, but a sharp pain shot through her right ankle. The appendage refused to support her weight. On hands and knees, she crawled over the black rocks and back into the tiny cave.

Kelly unwrapped the pullover. The sweatshirt had miraculously remained tied around her waist, and helped cushion her fall into the rocks. She took a few sips of water, forcing herself to conserve the precious liquid, and nibbled at the bread. She shivered again and slipped the sweatshirt back on.

"Becky!" Kelly called again into the desert night. "Becky! Come back!"

A wave of pain engulfed her and she was shocked to feel a rush of fluid soak through her pants. Then a dizzying pain wracked her body.

"Becky!" The sound of her voice trailed away, lost in the stiffening wind. Wet and cold, she needed the Navajo blanket that had fallen during the horse's frantic retreat. She knew it was out by the rattler, at least twenty yards away. So, she started crawling.

52

KATE AND COOPER WATCHED the area around the cabin fill with a swarm of Search and Rescue personnel, both professionals and volunteers. Cars and trucks and handlers with horses and dogs all waited for instructions. Two helicopters flew low overhead working in a checkerboard pattern. Despite the darkness, the pilots continued combing the area using large searchlights, the beams skittering off the uneven desert landscape.

Cooper's phone rang. He answered and listened. "Got it." He slipped the phone back into his pocket. "Sanders says our interview with Buck wasn't very thorough."

"Because ...?" Kate asked.

"Because Carl James, our dead *SP Trainline* subscriber, worked for the Southern Pacific. Buddy says he was canned a few months before he died. Apparently, he had a penchant for drinking on the job."

"Should we contact the Psychic Hotline to see if he derailed the train?"

"Always the wiseass. And there's something else you'll appreciate. No group called the Sons of Gestapo officially exists."

"Wonderful. We're finally getting some correlations that work, because Ramm doesn't exist either." Kate watched three riders mount up. A hound dog mix paced excitedly behind the horses. "By the way, where'd you get all these people on such short notice?"

"A state like Arizona really counts on its volunteers. There are such vast tracts of wilderness that when people go missing, we just can't cover all the open areas without help. The police don't have the manpower. These people," Cooper nodded toward the three horsemen, "bring their own vehicles and horses and dogs and backwoods expertise. In situations like this, we'd be hard-pressed to function without them."

A man sitting at a table by a large white van waved Cooper over. He pulled off a pair of headphones and rested them on his neck. "The boys in the copters say they have to call it a night. The wind is getting shifty. There's a storm coming. It's too dangerous."

"Have 'em head in," Cooper said. "But tell them to be back here ready to go at dawn."

"Will do."

"Wait a minute. Can any of the pilots land anywhere near here?"

"Let me check." A few moments later the van man said, "Down near the mine. There's a flat area just to the east. Sam's finishing his run. He'll meet you there in about thirty minutes."

"Thanks."

Cooper and Kate walked toward the cabin, past three volunteers manning a table filled with refreshments. The deputy grabbed a shiny glazed donut with a generous smear of chocolate icing. He finished it off in three bites.

"Say nothing, Butler."

"Yes, sir."

Inside the cabin, Kate and Cooper were greeted by the aroma of what smelled like spicy meat. Elect Sun sat next to Ramm. Elect Peter and Deputy Fielding sat opposite each other, spooning what looked to be chili from white ceramic bowls. Fielding looked up sheepishly when Cooper entered.

"Any word on Kelly?" Elect Sun rose and gathered two more bowls from the sideboard.

"I'm afraid not." Cooper glanced at Ramm. "Has your friend said anything new that might help us find her?"

Elect Sun placed two steaming bowls of the fragrant concoction on the table. Cooper pulled out a chair for Kate then sat next to her.

"I thought you were vegetarians," Cooper said, after tasting the dish.

"We are," Elect Peter assured him.

"But this is chili." Kate ate another spoonful of the spicy dish. "It's delicious."

"Meatless, I assure you." Elect Sun settled wearily on a chair.

"Why do you accuse me?" Ramm's voice startled everyone at the table.

"The girl was here. You took her from the train," Cooper tried to control his anger. "You bought her clothes. And there's blood on your carpet and in your truck. I'm guessing both samples belong to Kelly Garcia. So why don't you just tell us where you dumped her?"

Elect Sun gasped. "No, no! You're wrong. He would not hurt her."

"Can you truly believe *I* would harm a child?" Ramm didn't give Cooper time to answer. "Let the little children come to me, and do not forbid them; for such is the kingdom of heaven."

"Oh, cram it!" Cooper pushed away from the table and walked toward the door.

Elect Sun buried her face in her hands.

Cooper stopped and turned around. "I don't especially care who you think you are. What I do care about is a lost pregnant teenager. I'm going to need your fingerprints."

Something deep inside Ramm's fractured mind screamed that he should resist, and that, under the circumstances, he did not have to comply. He had yet to be charged with a crime. But part of him wanted all of this—all the years of hiding, pretending— to finally end. He held out his hands. "Do as you wish."

Cooper opened the front door and disappeared. Moments later, a short bald man, wearing glasses and sporting a Yuma County Sheriff's Department windbreaker, entered the room with what looked like a metal notebook.

"Gil, right here." Cooper singled out Ramm. "Mr. Ramm just gave us permission to take his prints."

Ramm's fingertips were smeared through the dark ink and pressed into prepared forms, one print to each box. Vivid blue-black splotches filled the card. Gilbert Armena signed and dated the forms.

"Thanks." Gil nodded, closed the notebook, and left the cabin.

53

THE HELICOPTER, WHIRLING blades slicing singular music, sang through the desert night.

"No!" Ramm covered both ears with his hands.

The anguished cry stopped Cooper as he approached the front door. The deputy turned and watched the man rock back and forth as the chopper came closer. Elect Sun jumped to Ramm's aid. The woman wrapped one arm around his shoulder, and spoke in a soothing manner to ease his fears.

"No! I will not do this again!" Ramm jumped from his seat, knocking a bowl of chili to the floor. He pushed Elect Sun away. She staggered toward the sideboard.

"Can't you do something for him?" she implored Elect Peter. "Give him something!"

"He's already had the Haloperidol. But it doesn't work instantly. Give it some time." Elect Peter slowly approached Ramm who was now crouched in the corner of the living room, hands still covering his ears.

"Fielding." Cooper addressed the young officer who still sat at the table too stunned to move. "Help them get Ramm to bed, and keep an eye on things."

"Ye … yes, sir." Fielding gazed down at what was left of his chili.

"Now!"

Cooper and Kate watched the helicopter land on the tiny flat space east of the mine site.

"Find anything?" Cooper asked when the rotors finally slowed, and he and Kate had safely approached the bird.

"Nada," the pilot answered. "We'll get started again at daybreak. There's still a lot of ground to cover."

"I hope you don't mind taking this into Phoenix for me. I know you've already had a long day."

"Where's it going?" The pilot accepted the manila envelope. He put the package in a lockbox beside him.

"Downtown to the Phoenix PD. I'll have an officer waiting for you when you land. Just hand it over."

"Okay, I should be able to get there in about twenty minutes. The winds are being freaky, so don't hold me to it."

"Get it there when you can." Cooper waved as he and Kate scurried back out of the way.

The rotors began to move again, slowly at first, producing the whop-whop sound that morphed into a heavy hum as the speed increased. The pilot waved, and then disappeared, obscured as a cloud of desert dust whipped and swirled from the ground. Then the helicopter lifted up as lightly as an insect, and darted out into the night sky.

Cooper's phone rang. "You're kidding? I'll head over right now."

"What's up?" Kate yawned.

"We keeping you awake?" Cooper strode quickly toward the Blazer.

"I haven't had much sleep lately." She kept pace with him. "Or maybe I had too much on your couch. Anyway, don't worry about me."

"I won't."

They both got into the vehicle, slammed the doors, and buckled their seatbelts almost in unison.

"Where are we—"

But Cooper didn't let her finish. "We're going to the Children's compound. It seems there's been a sighting."

"Elvis?" Kate yawned again.

"Even better. The Virgin Mary." Cooper slipped the truck into gear and stepped on the gas.

Kate turned toward him, cocking her head. "Don't you think we should alert Search and Rescue?"

"It'll only take us a few minutes to drive over to the compound. Let's see what we've got first. You'll see what I mean when we get there. Trust me."

54

WHEN THE SCREEN DOOR opened, Cooper and Kate found themselves facing the tiny shriveled form of Elect Sarah, her usual smile replaced by a look of deep concern.

"Elect Sarah." Cooper greeted the blind woman. "It's Deputy Cooper. Kate Butler is also with me."

The woman nodded and, with a struggle, turned her walker around to lead them through the living room past the piano and drum set. The room held a faint odor of sour milk and overcooked vegetables.

"Thank you for coming so quickly," Elect Sarah said as they inched their way toward the kitchen.

Cooper was surprised to see the dishes overflowing in the sink, and pots and pans still holding the remains of the evening meal on the stove.

"You must excuse us." The blind woman apparently read his mind. "I know things are rather untidy right now. You see we depend on Elect Sun and Elect Peter quite a bit."

"No problem. Things look fine." Cooper lied.

"I'm sure they don't. But thank you for saying so."

"Elect Sarah. Where are all the others?

"I'll explain that in a minute. First, I need to tell you about Nunzio."

"No need," Cooper said. "I already know him."

Kate cast him a dark look. "But I don't."

"Nunzio is an elderly man who lives ... well ... all around here, dear." Elect Sarah waved one frail, freckled hand.

"He's homeless." Cooper turned to Kate. "But Nunzio isn't as destitute as someone who's living on the streets in Phoenix. He and his horse are fixtures around here. He does odd jobs for food. And the Children often help him out, though they don't approve of his fondness for tequila."

"Yes, he does drink heavily." Elect Sarah finally stepped through the kitchen doorway. "But he is a kind man, and we do what we can to help him."

"And Nunzio is here now with some information for us?" Cooper tried to move the conversation forward.

Elect Sarah lowered herself into one of the green wooden kitchen chairs, and took a deep breath. "Nunzio came to tell us that he saw ... the Virgin Mary out in the desert. That he gave her food and water, and left her a gold nugget. Gifts for her and her child."

"Has he been drinking?" Cooper asked.

"Yes." Elect Sarah focused her cloudy gaze over his head. "But with Kelly missing, can we afford to discount what he said?"

"No, of course not."

"Did he say he saw a baby?" Kate shuddered at the thought of the young girl alone giving birth in the desert.

"No, Nunzio said the Holy Mother was with child. I took that to mean she was pregnant. He's out back. They're all out back."

Kate and Cooper found Nunzio and the other members of the Children of Light, out in the yard praying. Though their religious beliefs differed, they prayed with equal fervor. While the Children asked God for the safe return of the young girl and the baby they soon hoped to know, Nunzio ran his gnarled fingers down the wooden beads of the rosary he hadn't touched in years, and prayed zealously for his immortal soul.

55

THE AREA AROUND the cabin was finally quiet. The members of the Search and Rescue team who chose to remain so they could get an early start were bedded down in trucks and vans and tents. The horses were corralled, and the dogs—valued for their tracking skills, but also loved as family pets—snuggled up next to their masters. Inside the cabin, Elect Sun slept quietly on the couch, while Elect Peter, sprawled across the armchair and ottoman, snored fitfully.

Deputy Fielding sat next to the door outside of Ramm's room, and hoped the discomfort caused by the straight-back wooden chair would keep him awake. With the door slightly cracked, Fielding could hear Ramm's uneven breathing. He also noticed the wind outside as small objects periodically plinked against the house. Fielding yawned and blinked his eyes, then got up and headed into the kitchen where he knew a pot of strong, probably lukewarm, coffee sat on the stove.

ψ

In the bedroom, Ramm bolted up, eyes wide, sweat staining the T-shirt and shorts he had no memory of changing into. He slipped out of bed and cautiously moved toward the window, his senses telling him something wasn't right. Heavy steps sounded outside the bedroom door. Silently, Ramm moved back to the bed, sliding beneath the covers.

When everything was quiet again, Ramm edged his way toward the slightly open door. He could only see the lower half of the man's legs; still he knew it was a police officer camped outside.

A sound distracted him. Ramm peaked through the vertical opening, and saw Elect Peter snoring in the chair. Retreating to the far side of the bedroom, he considered his options.

Thoughts flashed into his mind in jumbled order.

Searchers were coming and going from his property. He remembered the pain of the spider bite, and the strange peace—the same warm, honey-colored feeling he'd known in Jerusalem—that had engulfed him. The girl happily modeling the clothes he'd purchased for her. Suddenly, he realized he had no idea where Kelly was. The faint smudges on his fingers distracted him, and Ramm remembered with devastating clarity that he had willingly allowed the deputy to take his fingerprints. How long ago had that occurred? He had lost all track of time. But his mind was clearer now. He recalled that Elect Peter had dosed him with Haloperidol.

A familiar whinny wrested Ramm from his thoughts. Creeping to the window, he saw Becky, a crudely knotted rope dangling around her neck, standing off in the trees that were writhing in the wind. The Appaloosa sniffed the air that was filled with unfamiliar scents of men and dogs and horses. She pawed the ground.

Silently, Ramm changed into a black T-shirt and a pair of dark camouflage pants. He laced up the heavy black boots.

Dog looked up at him from the floor and whined.

Ramm moved silently behind the door, and waited as Deputy Fielding slipped his head inside. Ramm grabbed the man. His first impulse was to snap the policeman's neck. Wide-eyed with terror, Fielding kicked and twisted in Ramm's steel grip. Something made Ramm change his mind. He dragged Fielding to the bed, grabbed a pillow, and jammed it into the deputy's face.

A short time later, the thrashing calmed. Ramm removed the pillow; the deputy's breath came in ragged gasps. Ramm paused and looked at the officer who appeared not much older than a boy. He'd killed so many people, what was one more? He lifted the pillow again, but dropped it and smashed his fist into the side of Fielding's face. A broken jaw and a concussion would keep him out for a while. He covered the young cop with the blankets.

Ramm strapped the thick blade to his thigh, then reached into the lower dresser drawer, and peeled off a thin package that had been taped to the wood above. He folded the envelope in half and zipped the money and multiple identification papers in a pants pocket. Ramm paused for a moment, heard nothing, and moved to the window. Slowly, he eased the pane open, but stopped when Dog began to whine again. Knowing she would bark if left behind, he grabbed the animal, hoisted her up, and dropped her to the ground outside the window.

56

KATE SAT ACROSS the kitchen table from Nunzio, doing her best to sober him up. She poured another cup of strong black coffee. Cooper remained outside where he spoke with the rest of the Children in the hope that Nunzio might have said something about the location where he had encountered the "Holy Mother."

Fifteen minutes later, Cooper pushed open the screen door and let it snap shut behind him. "Kelly may be somewhere along Windmill Wash, but I can't be sure." He turned to Nunzio. "You can help me." The old man took another sip of coffee, and stared back through watery eyes. Cooper tried again. "Tell me exactly where you saw the girl."

"The Holy Mother is by the black rocks, like I told you." Nunzio pushed the mug toward Kate. "Don't you have just a little tequila? I know it will clear my head."

"Black rocks. Which black rocks?" Cooper pulled out a chair and sat between them. "It's a big desert and practically all the rocks out here are black. Nothing but black basalt everywhere you look. Give me something to go on. The girl might be in danger."

Nunzio's eyes widened. "Danger? Who would hurt the Holy Mother?"

Cooper took the cue. "There are coyotes out there. Mountain lions. Rattlers."

"Perhaps you could lead us to her." Kate pushed the coffee mug back. "Wouldn't you like to see her again?"

Nunzio frowned. Kate realized the thought of seeing his version of the Virgin frightened him. She'd said the wrong thing.

Wind lashed the side of the house.

"A storm is coming in, Nunzio." Kate changed tack. "We must get to her to keep her safe. Keep the baby safe. Won't you help us find her?"

The old man paused and stared into the coffee cup. Then, finally, he stood and steadied himself with both hands on the table. "I will!" He walked toward the door. "I will take you to her. The three of us will find the little mother. Just like the Great Kings of the East."

A short time later, the Blazer crawled behind Nunzio, even though he moved faster and with more determination than he had in years.

"Just go with it." Kate saw the frustration eating away at Cooper.

"Why can't he just get in the truck like a normal person?" Cooper growled as Nunzio, with the roan in tow, left the dirt trail and cut across the open desert. "I have four-wheel drive. I can go wherever he wants."

"Pull over." Kate reached for the door handle.

"Pull over? This ain't I-10. You're allowed to just stop anywhere you want when you're traveling without the benefit of a real road."

Kate tilted her head. "It's just a figure of speech. Quit being cranky and stop. I'll go keep him company and see if I can get him moving."

"Remind me." Cooper said as she opened the door. "Which one of the three kings are you?"

"I am Xena, Warrior Princess. Which means someday when I grow up, I'll be Xena Warrior Queen. And that's about as close as I'm gonna get."

"Oh, Xena! Any time you want to don that leather bustier and those breast plates and boots, give me a call."

"Certainly." Kate grinned. "And then I will kick your ass. Now leave me, commoner. I have work to do."

An hour later, frustrated from driving at a crawl and unable to sustain the image of Kate dressed in Xena garb, Cooper stopped the Blazer just as the police radio came on.

"Coop! It's Buddy. It seems Christ has risen."

"What?"

"Ramm attacked Fielding and took off. The kid can hardly talk. He's got a broken jaw and a concussion."

"How long has Ramm been gone?" Cooper rolled down the window and waved Kate back to the truck.

"We're not really sure. Elect Sun woke up and found Fielding unconscious under the covers in Ramm's bed. She alerted the Search and Rescue guys who were camped out there. They called it in."

A gust of wind blasted the Blazer, buffeting the truck with pieces of rock and sand. Cooper scanned the horizon. In the east, lit by the moon, he saw the reddish dust rising hundreds of feet into the sky. "Shit! Looks like we've got a haboob heading our way. Damn! We're tracking Nunzio back to where he says he saw the girl, and I was just going to ask you to send out the choppers."

"Nunzio? That sounds like an adventure."

"Trust me, it is. Can you get the guys airborne?"

"I'm not sure. We'll check out the storm and do what we can."

"Hey, Buddy. Do we know if Ramm's armed?"

"Negative. We just have to assume he is. Now, give me your location and I'll roust Search and Rescue and send you some backup."

57

RAMM MANAGED TO SLIP past the sleeping searchers by leading the Appaloosa up over the rise behind the cabin. Once they were a good distance away, he checked the horse for injuries. Finding none, he mounted up.

It would be impossible to track Kelly properly from the cabin without being seen, so all he could do was make an educated guess. The girl had only been on a few short walks outside, all to the area just below the Rowley Mine.

Because of his need to skirt the cabin, an hour passed before Ramm reached the wash. Once there, he examined the edges of the streambed where small stones rested in a plethora of white sand. It would be here on the sides of the wash—away from the center where large tumbled rocks cluttered the area—that he might be able to discern which way Kelly had gone.

Ramm got down on his hands and knees, and studied various depressions in the moonlight. A number of horses had been in the wash recently. Trackers probably, but not Becky.

Without warning, the light was extinguished. Ramm looked up. Fast moving clouds darted across the sky obscuring the moon. Then the clouds skipped away and the luminosity returned. Ramm saw the storm coming in hard from the east—a great roiling cloud blotting out everything in its wake. The wind was harsh now. He could smell earthy odors coming from above where they didn't belong. Ramm had to work fast, but tracking wasn't a process that could be hurried.

Finally, a hoof print caught his eye. He pressed his face close to the ground. The sand was harder here and it held the print well. He found what he was looking for— the nick. Ramm had carved small grooves into Becky's shoes—all at three o'clock—so she'd be easy to track if she ever got loose. He saw another print and then another and discerned where the horse had traveled up over the edge of the wash.

Ramm moved more quickly now, concerned the dust storm would rip the tracks and any other clues from the ground, send them spiraling into the air, eliminating all hope of finding the girl before daylight. He noticed a broken branch hanging from a palo verde tree, one that had grown low to the ground and could have easily been snapped by a horse's hoof. He checked the broken edges. A fresh cut.

Ramm climbed the rocky slope. No longer in the protected confines of the wash, he was hit hard by a gust of wind; still he guided the horse in a straight line past scraggly mesquite, unforgiving fields of cholla, and a few scattered saguaros including one exceptionally large cactus with myriad limbs.

Then he heard something. Dog barked and bolted. Ramm tried to filter out the extraneous noises, but the wind was too intense. He kicked the Appaloosa sharply with his heels and followed the dog.

Ramm kept pace with the animal as she raced toward a pile of boulders. Then a *CRACK* split the air. Becky reared. Ramm clung to the horse, lying flat. *Was someone shooting at him?* But when Becky spun around, Ramm saw the giant saguaro. He watched the cactus tilt in a slow-motion fall to the rocky ground, shallow roots no longer able to bear such massive weight in the face of the oncoming haboob. The ancient monster had finally given up its hold in the earth, and the crash was like the downing of a small plane. The giant shaft split apart, scattering broken limbs across the desert floor.

A piercing scream broke through the gale and dragged Ramm's attention away from the ruined cactus. He leapt from the horse and sprinted toward the rocks without his usual caution. Dog appeared ghostlike out of the darkness, barked, and disappeared again. Wind roared in Ramm's ears like an oncoming train.

58

COOPER ROLLED DOWN the window and leaned his head out. "Hey! Hold up!" But his voice was drowned out by the wind, so he jumped out and ran after them.

It wasn't until Cooper grabbed Kate by the arm that she knew he was there. With his mouth inches from her ear he yelled, "Get in the truck!"

Kate pointed ahead to Nunzio. The old man, undaunted by the storm, led the horse in the hazy, reddish glow created by the swirling dust and the Blazer's headlights. They watched as he scanned the horizon, the vagaries of the storm, for the moment, permitting a clear view of the land to the west. Nunzio shook his head, stopped and then led the roan back toward the truck.

"It's not here. But I know this is where it should be," Nunzio's gravelly voice was filled with anguish.

"What are you looking for?" Cooper shouted.

Nunzio ignored him and looked up into the howling sky. "God! Help me find the Holy Mother." He fell to his knees, pulled his rosary from his pocket, and began to pray.

Cooper grabbed the man by the shoulders. "Let's go! Get in the truck where we can sort this out."

Nunzio stared at Cooper, confusion etched on his craggy face.

"Should've given him that shot of tequila," Kate yelled. Looping her arm through his, she eased Nunzio off the ground, and helped him to the truck.

Cooper slammed the door shutting out the din, then ran his fingers through his windswept hair. "What are we looking for exactly?" He turned to the backseat where the old man perched fingering the rosary.

Kate saw Nunzio's cloudy eyes fill with tears. She placed her hand on his weathered brown arm to calm him.

"The Holy Mother is by the black rocks." He rubbed one of the small beads—the type signifying the Hail Mary prayer—between his thumb and forefinger.

"Here we go again." Cooper hit his hand on the steering wheel.

"Think, Nunzio. Which black rocks?" Kate asked in a soothing voice.

"The ones behind the ancient saguaro," he said as if a cloud had suddenly lifted. "It is extremely old. Maybe thirty limbs. I have passed it many times, and have used it as a landmark. I know the Holy Mother is near it, in a small cave hidden by the black rocks." Nunzio sat back in the seat, clutching the rosary to his chest.

"Cooper!" Buddy's voice blasted from the police radio. "Choppers are on the way. Though the storm is making things pretty hairy. Some areas are clear. Some totally obscured."

"What are the weather wonks saying?" Cooper peered out the windshield at the frenetic cloud of reddish dust.

"You know how those guys are. This one caught them by surprise. Hell! Too late in the season for this kind of storm."

"Tough job forecasting the weather in southern Arizona." Kate watched the towering storm roll over them. "What do they have? Maybe twenty days a year where it's not hot and sunny?"

"The storm should pass out of the area within the hour," Buddy said. "And, before you go, I heard from the lab in Phoenix. While it'll be a while before they have absolute confirmation, a cursory comparison of the prints you took and the ones the military had on file show our boy is definitely *not* Jason Ramm."

59

RAMM FELL TO HIS KNEES beside her. "Kelly, I'm here." His voice was low and calming. "You're going to be okay. We're going to get through this."

Eyes wild with terror, she reached out and clenched onto his arm, her fingers like a vise as another wave of pain engulfed her.

Ramm smoothed Kelly's hair as she bit her lip and arched her back, fighting against the pain.

"Don't fight it. You have to make the pain work for you." He had never delivered a baby, but he knew what to do. He pulled a small flashlight out of a pocket and set it on the ground so he could see. Then he froze.

Kelly's pants were wet, soaked with blood. Disjointed images flooded his mind. The faces of victims appeared and disappeared. To his horror, the dead kept opening their eyes, looking back at him, alive, no matter how many times he pulled the trigger, or slid a knife through their necks.

He wrenched out of Kelly's grasp and pressed his back against the wall of the shallow cave. He covered his face with his hands as the blond boy appeared, as always wreathed in black smoke, emerging for the thousandth time from the fire. "Kill me!" the boy screamed. Ramm pulled the trigger, but the boy would not die. He just kept coming, eyes melting from their sockets. "Kill me!" he begged again and again. "Kill me!"

"No!" Ramm pulled at his hair and shook his head. "I won't do it! I can't!"

"Help me, Jason! Please!" Kelly reached out and her fingers grazed his arm.

He flinched and turned toward her voice. Then he blinked, the burning boy evaporated along with the black smoke, and her face appeared.

Ramm drew a ragged breath. Then another. Instinct took over. "I'm sorry, Kelly. I'm here. I'm here … I promise."

Gingerly, he slid Kelly's pants off and rolled them into a pillow to cushion her head. She'd been sitting on Becky's blanket so he slid her down on her back and immediately saw the crown of the baby's head."

"When you feel a contraction, you need to push. Use your muscles. Don't hold back."

She nodded as she clenched her jaw in pain. Kelly closed her eyes and grunted through the contraction. When the pain momentarily passed, she looked up at Jason, tears streaming down her face. "Don't be angry. I tried to get help, but I wrecked your truck. I don't know how to drive! So, I took Becky, but then a snake scared her and she ran away and—"

"That's all over." He wiped her forehead with his sleeve. "I'm here now."

"Are you okay?" She placed a warm palm on his cheek.

In that instant, Ramm felt the now-familiar calm spread through him. Part of him wanted to fight the feeling, part wanted to give in to the sensation. Then he heard them coming. In the distance, the air thrummed with that awful sound, vibrations cutting through him like serrated steel. His head pounded. He left Kelly's side and edged up over the rocks. If some were coming by air, there'd be others on foot.

Kelly screamed, an unearthly sound coming from deep inside as a contraction seized hold of her.

He looked back. "Quiet!"

She screamed against the pain and pushed hard.

Frantic, Ramm took his place beside her again, eyes still focused on the entrance to the tiny cave. "Please! You must be quiet or they'll find us."

Kelly's eyes widened in confusion. She shook her head frantically. When Ramm stared at the girl, he was appalled to find his hands covering her mouth. Kelly fought, still he held her down, blocking her screams.

Finally, Ramm released his grip and pulled back, horrified by what he had done. Kelly coughed and wheezed as she drew air into her lungs. "Forgive me." He moved to take hold of the child. Ramm gazed at the infant whose blood-covered body emerged, and he knew he had finally found the one who could save him. Tears streamed down his dirt-encrusted cheeks as he cradled the child's head and upper torso in his hands. The words from Revelation came to him:

And behold, I am coming quickly, and my reward is with me, to give to everyone according to his work.

What reward could he expect to receive for his life's work? A life of death and pain.

Kelly gave one last push, and the child slipped into Ramm's waiting hands.

The helicopters were almost on top of them now. But there was still time to beg for forgiveness. This child could heal his wounded soul. All he had to do was ask.

A cold shock wave washed over him. He stared at the girl-child and his dream of forgiveness evaporated, blown to bits like the swirling desert dust. He looked from the child to the sweat-soaked mother who lay panting on the horse blanket. Not the Madonna, after all.

It was no good. There would be no pardon for him. Devastated, Ramm fell back into medic mode. He cleared the mucous from the baby's mouth and made sure she was breathing properly. Then he placed the infant into Kelly's arms and tucked the oversized sweatshirt around them both.

The *whump whump whump* of rotors whirled above them and two searchlights scanned the ground, bouncing wildly over the rocks.

"Are they here for you?" Kelly asked.

Ramm nodded, then leaned over and kissed her on the forehead. He stood. The dog, huddled at the back of the cave, rose, and stared at Ramm. "No, Dog! Stay!" The animal inched over and lay by the girl. "Hold her collar. If you can. Keep her with you."

Kelly nodded.

"Don't worry. They'll find you here. Very soon. You're going to be fine."

Then Jason Ramm stepped out of the cave, gazed up at the choppers that were being buffeted by the whirling red dust, and took one last look at Kelly. He nodded at her and disappeared into the storm.

60

WEEKS PASSED.

There was no sign of Jason Ramm. Kelly and her healthy, seven-pound baby girl spent one night in a local hospital and then went home to stay with the Children of Light.

Initially, Miranda Garcia balked at having her misshapen daughter back in the area, but she unexpectedly stopped complaining, and suddenly disappeared after packing her possessions and driving off in a brand-new convertible.

One day, to Elect Sun's astonishment, she opened the back door to find Ramm's Appaloosa tied under the old cottonwood tree. The animal, originally taken in by a member of the Search and Rescue squad, was purchased from the man one week later by someone unknown to him. The very same day the horse arrived, a carpenter appeared with prepaid work orders to construct a small barn and a corral on the Children's property.

Elect Sun was shocked again when Garfield Jessup arrived one beautiful fall morning. The wiry, mustachioed man in the three-piece suit smiled as he introduced himself as Elect Sun's attorney. Though she protested, insisting she had no lawyer—nor any reason to need one—Jessup kept smiling. "It's all worked out," he assured her.

A tutor had been arranged for Kelly. And, Jessup explained, if the girl did well, she could use her college fund to go anywhere in the country she wanted. In the meantime, an account had been set up to provide for her and the baby. Jessup then handed Elect Sun the name, address, and phone number of a doctor in California who specialized in facial surgery for people afflicted with Moebius Syndrome. Though the final decision in that regard was up to Kelly. Also, an eye doctor would be calling to examine Elect Sarah. Perhaps all she needed was cataract surgery.

Next came the deed to the land surrounding and including the Rowley Mine. When Kelly turned eighteen, the land and the cabin would belong to her. Jessup then reached into his briefcase and removed a velvet box, which he handed to the girl. Inside was her father's Silver Star.

The final piece of news concerned one more bank account, this one in the name of the Children of Light. It contained two million dollars. Jessup explained he had been retained to make sure both accounts were managed wisely.

At first, Elect Sun struggled with the windfall. The Children believed money caused much of the world's evil. In the end, she agreed to keep the funds when Jessup assured her the Children were free to use the money any way they pleased. As it happened, whenever something was needed in Hyder or Agua Caliente or the surrounding area, like money for an operation, or a new roof, or a college education, the funds magically appeared with no strings attached.

Elect Sun was known to say that this "gift from God" would bring light into the lives of their neighbors.

EPILOGUE

ONE YEAR AFTER the wreck of the Sunset Limited, a child searching for firewood came across some bones in South Vietnam just east of the Cambodian border. The man was identified through dental records. Forensic experts agreed the soldier had been severely burned, but that had not been the cause of the man's death. One neatly placed bullet between the soldier's eyes had ended his young life. That the bullet had come from an American weapon was disappointing, but since friendly fire deaths often occurred, and the soldier had no living relatives, the military found no reason to release that bit of information

With much ceremony, the soldier was transported to Phoenix, then airlifted by helicopter to an open field not far from a spot where hot springs once bubbled out of the Sonoran Desert ground. A full honor guard carried the flag-draped casket on the short walk to the Agua Caliente Pioneer Cemetery.

Kate and Cooper watched from the edge of the small gathering.

"I wonder who he was. Why pretend to be this man?" Kate asked as they watched the casket being lowered into the ground next to the grave of Alexander Ramm, the itinerant preacher who befriended the Children of Light so many years earlier.

Cooper shook his head. "I don't know."

The crowd that turned out to honor the boy who had given his life for his country so long ago was silent as the soldiers aimed their rifles into the bright fall sky, the salvos echoing off the nearby basalt mountain. Among the mourners were Elect Sun and Elect Peter who had cherished the motherless boy and who had figured prominently in the countless stories the young man had told his best friend while they served side by side in Vietnam.

Now, after thirty years in a shallow foreign grave, Jason Ramm was finally home, and his friend had once again disappeared.

NOTES

The facts surrounding the wreck of the Amtrak Sunset Limited are true. However, I have taken literary license on two counts. The train, which was derailed during the early-morning hours of October 9, 1995, was heading toward Los Angeles, but was east of Hyder when it plunged off the tracks. Also, there is no train station in Hyder. There was a stop in the tiny town years ago, but it has long since been closed. Other than these two discrepancies, the newsworthy events leading up to the derailment, including the burning of the Southern Pacific Railroad trestle, the discovery of dynamite in the gas station restroom, and the derailment itself are as they occurred.

All of the characters in *A Light in the Desert* are fictitious with the exception of the following people.

Mitchell Bates, an Amtrak employee, died in the crash. Dr. Yair Bar El was the first to clinically identify the Jerusalem Syndrome and is the former head of the psychiatric hospital Kfur Shaul in Israel. Sheriff Joe Arpaio was the long-time sheriff of Arizona's Maricopa County. John Signor authored the historical article on the deadly 1939 Harney, Nevada derailment in SP Trainline. In 1909,

Mrs. H. Rowley, along with her husband, put a claim on the Arizona mine that bears their name. David Koresh, the self-proclaimed Messiah and leader of the Branch Davidians, was killed along with 75 of his followers by federal forces during a shootout and subsequent fire at his compound in Waco, Texas in 1993. All other characters in the book are of my own creation and are meant to bear no resemblance to anyone living or dead.

At the date of this writing, the wreck of the Amtrak Sunset Limited remains an unsolved crime.

ACKNOWLEDGMENT

I would like to extend my appreciation to everyone who helped me complete *A Light in the Desert*. First, I'd like to thank my agent, Donna Eastman of Parkeast Literary Agency, for her patience, guidance, and belief in me. Kristina Makansi at Amphora Publishing Group not only served as my editor – a position that never gets the credit it truly deserves – she also designed the cover. Thank you, Kristy, for wearing both hats on this project. I'd also like to thank my fabulous group of beta readers who, in this case, ferreted out all those errors that skipped past me. To Marissa De Santiago, Mary Jo West, Dr. Susan Taffer, Kim Sivey, and Dr. Laurie Rappl thank you for catching my mistakes. I am especially grateful to the Children of Light for enduring my questions as they endeavored to explain their beliefs to me. I would like to thank the people at what was formerly the Arizona Mining and Mineral Museum for their guidance and the librarians at the Saguaro Branch of the Phoenix Public Library. Special thanks go to Maricopa County Deputy Sheriff Dave Woolley, one of the first to arrive at the scene of the wreck of the Amtrak Sunset Limited, and to my dear late friend Don Clarkson for his stories about Vietnam. Finally, my heartfelt thanks to Ryan Pickard for accompanying me on those trips to Hyder and always having a sense of humor when he did.

ABOUT THE AUTHOR

Anne Butler Montgomery has worked as a television sportscaster, newspaper and magazine writer, teacher, amateur baseball umpire, and high school football referee. Her first TV job came at WRBL-TV in Columbus, Georgia, and led to positions at WROC-TV in Rochester, New York, KTSP-TV in Phoenix, Arizona, and ESPN in Bristol, Connecticut, where she anchored the Emmy and ACE award-winning *SportsCenter*. She finished her on-camera broadcasting career with a two-year stint as the studio host for the NBA's Phoenix Suns. Montgomery was a freelance and/or staff reporter for six publications, writing sports, features, movie reviews, and archeological pieces. Her novels include: *The Scent of Rain, A Light in the Desert* and the forthcoming *Nothing But Echoes*. Montgomery teaches journalism at South Mountain High School in Phoenix, is a foster mom to three sons, and is an Arizona Interscholastic Association football referee and crew chief. When she can, she indulges in her passions: rock collecting, football officiating, scuba diving, and playing her guitar.

CPSIA information can be obtained
at www.ICGtesting.com
Printed in the USA
LVHW04s1549280918
591695LV00005B/6/P